To Jur

I'm so glad to

have spent the

SEARCHING FOR SUZI

last 2 years at

Naropa! Thank

you _so_ much

for all your

support!

Nancy

12-11-09

SEARCHING FOR SUZI

a flash novel

Nancy Stohlman

Monkey Puzzle Press
Boulder, Colorado

Copyright © 2009 by Nancy Stohlman

Cover Photo by Andrew J. Baran

Cover & Book Design by Nate Jordon

ISBN 0-9801650-6-7

Monkey Puzzle Press
3116 47th St.
Boulder, CO   80301

www.monkeypuzzleonline.com

I

It's not like she had some profound impact on my life. Yes, she was my first female lover, so I guess that counts for something, but in a life that turned out mostly heterosexual it hardly was a turning point. And considering the last interaction we had was at a strip club, her accusing me of stealing her mother's stainless steel goulash pot (which I did, but only as payback), we didn't leave on warm terms. So why now, after seventeen years, did I give a shit about finding Suzi Cooper?

It started with a dream: I was back at the Sugar Lounge. Suzi and all the others were still working there. No one had aged or changed and my entrance into the bar was marked by cheers and hugs and kisses as if I was back for a family reunion with all my sisters.

I often have reoccurring dreams about strip clubs. I'm usually sneaking away from the house while my husband and sons are asleep like one of the Twelve Stripping Princesses in paper-thin heels and magic glitter gel, I arrive at some nameless club where I win a bunch of money and sneak home before dawn. Locations change, my costumes change.

But this dream was different. This time my husband and two young sons had followed me, parading into the bar right behind me, shaking hands with the bouncer as if he was Uncle Charlie, grenadine spritzers for the kiddies, my littlest stretching out for a nap under the cigarette smoke, porn playing on the big screen.

I thought about that dream over coffee. After seventeen years it seemed unlikely that I could return to the Sugar Lounge, or the Red Umbrella, or Dick's Yum Yum Club, or any of the places we once worked, to find Suzi. But I wanted to walk back in those clubs. Why? I didn't know. Perhaps it's the desire of an adult to drive by a childhood home once more, slowly, even after it's been long ago sold and repainted, just to remember the shape of a bedroom, the shag of the hallway carpet, how it felt to be ten years old looking out that upstairs window. And considering I was barely old enough to drive the first time I stepped through the Sugar Lounge's swinging door, returning there would be a bit like going home.

"You want a job, huh?" the big man with the swollen gut says to me. His dark tan contrasts with his white pompadour. "How old are you?"

"Twenty," I lie.

"Twenty, huh?" he says, looking me over. "Well then no drinking. Have you ever danced before?"

"No, but I'm a model."

He smiles, chewing on a toothpick. "You're a model, huh?" He says it like he doesn't believe me but doesn't care. "Let's get you upstairs and into a costume." He grabs a cocktail napkin and a pen from his coat pocket. "What's your name?"

I think of something and he writes it down, chuckling. "Follow me."

A mirrored ball spins white teardrops of light across a two-tiered stage where a dancer is sliding around a pole. A movie screen covers one whole wall. On the screen, two women rub shaving cream on each other's breasts. The boss elbows open a set of saloon-style swinging doors. "Joe, this is," he looks again at the napkin, "Natalie. Can you get her into a costume?"

The dressing room is fluorescent-lit and filled with lockers. A mirror traverses the length of one wall, reflecting abandoned curling irons coated with layers of crusted brown hairspray, tangled cords, and broken compact mirrors scattered across the makeup table. Chunks of eyeshadow and blush are ground into the formica.

Joe unlocks a storage closet and holds up a handful of

brightly colored strings and strips of cloth. I separate the rhinestones, tassels and lace. I'm going to follow through, this time.

Now adorned in burgundy sparkles. Cleavage deep and white, virginal, rub red lips together, comb through hair with shaky fingers, lips buzzing, adjust g-string between butt cheeks, air conditioning goosebumps on exposed skin, ignore baby fat still clinging to thighs, hips.

She is not me.

Natalie parts the beaded curtain.

Click, click, click up the stairs. It's lunchtime, so the club is empty except for one guy. The opening drum beats of "Sharp Dressed Man." Her hands are clammy against the brass pole as she tries to spin, almost flinging herself off the stage. All those pageant routines, all her perfect three-point catwalk turns—fucking useless. Mirrors are positioned around the stage in triplicate like in the changing rooms of big department stores—Natalie on Natalie on Natalie on Natalie looks jerky and embarrassed, pasty white, six different Natalies snap their fingers to *every girl's crazy 'bout a sharp dressed man* like fragmented pieces of herself bisecting, trisecting, severing from the original.

The lone customer stands and approaches the stage. Natalie kneels, thinking he's going to tell her she looks ridiculous, but instead he loops a bill through her shoulder strap.

Ten dollars just like that.

II

Black-Eyed Susans tangle along the sides of the interstate, choking each other for sunlight. The tops of corn tassels are beginning to turn, silken tufts ready. Sunflowers without petals bow their heads as you drive by, alone in your minivan.

Each town name is strangely familiar and every now and then a bend in the highway prickles you with recognition: Troy, Mound City, Rockport, Thank You for Visiting Missouri Please Come Again, Welcome to Iowa.

You near Council Bluffs and the exit for Offutt Air Force Base and wonder if your father still lives in that ostentatious house in his second unhappy marriage. Seems all those ribbons on his uniform didn't make his wife like him or make his daughter behave. Tabasco-sauce-on-the-tongue punishments, wooden spoon spankings for not rinsing out a cereal bowl, he lied about the affair he was having with the woman next door while your mother took to nursing old liquor bottles in the dark, trying to become an alcoholic (it failed). You tried to kill yourself at fifteen and when that didn't work, you moved out.

You're approaching the Omaha exits. You don't remember the Love Shack, an enormous new club off the side of the highway. It's right next to the XXX Adult Superstore, a windowless black building with metallic lettering: Porn! Porn! Porn! Midnight Videos. Open 24 Hours. Was that the one you went to with...?

A combination of instinct and memory tells you not to take the first exit into Omaha but to keep going and take the second, the one with the big view across the Missouri River, gushing brown and opaque beneath the skyline. Casinos sparkle along the river now, flashing advertisements and upcoming acts. The Woodman Tower, once lording above the skyline like a solitary penis, has been upstaged.

The trees have gotten so big, leafy monstrosities that make your memories seem smaller. You're driving on a road that you can't remember the name of but you clearly remember it's long, curvy stretch from your dreams, and you wonder which version of the street is more poignant, the real one or the dream one. You navigate on pure instinct. You recognize a gas station with a green sign that hasn't changed in twenty years, you *feel* it as the place to turn. And yes, there is your first apartment building. Well, it's not really your first because your first apartment was with that girl from high school—you slept on her broken waterbed and she slept on the couch and you lied about your age, even to her, and you let the upstairs neighbor go down on you just because he was older and bartended at the clubhouse next to the pool and you thought it might give you some status. But this, this was your first solo apartment, rented to you at age sixteen because no one bothered to check your ID, funny how often that was a theme then, and the tree in front has gotten so huge, the whole building is in gorgeous shade. This is also the apartment that was haunted, the one where you played the Ouija board too many times until that dancer named Sparkle, the weird, coked-out one that claimed she was a witch and would read your tarot cards on slow nights, she said you had let in the demons. This is the apartment that Suzi lived in for that month. She never paid rent and hardly ever slept in it, she just needed a place to store all her crap, and when she did sleep there it's not like the two of you had any romantic rendezvous, that was all over by then. You wanted to be in love with her but she didn't want to be in love with you; that was never her goal.

You pass the building slowly, then turn down a street you must have driven a hundred times, it feels as familiar as rolling over in bed, and you note the unchanged combination of rundown, antique, and functional shabby. People walk the streets with lunchtime hurry, more people than you remember, or maybe you were always too absorbed in yourself that you didn't notice, and you wonder if here, on these streets, was where you developed your love for dying city centers and rundown buildings.

There is a certain kind of memory embedded in these places. A kind of memory poured between bricks and mortar. We cannot alter it. We breathe and dream in a place and then it holds us, it remembers us. But it remembers us as we were. So to return is to become a fool, everything illuminated with the glow of nostalgia, a yellowing around the edges, a softening. Maybe that's the tragedy of living the same place all your life—you can't return. Leaving, which takes one sort of bravery, and then returning, which takes something completely different. Which repaints you. Bravery and humility in order to grow a person. Like the trees.

The cab drops Natalie in front of the Sugar Lounge, duffle bag in hand. Joe the bouncer towers half under the Sugar Lounge's purple awning and half in the open door. His suit is tailored, bald head shiny. Above him the neon silhouette of a woman flickers with low wattage. He looks at his watch disapprovingly as Natalie zooms past him and into the club, waving at the bartender and two of the regulars: Lou, the rich cowboy who always comes on Thursdays and tips $20s when he gets drunk, and the chemistry professor in the corner. They're auditioning a new girl on stage. She's clearly never danced before—the stiffness, the overdone *Flashdance* moves. Natalie remembers her own audition and her cheeks warm with embarrassment.

Upstairs, half-dressed dancers slam lockers and apply melted chunks of cheap lipstick. The club has a particular smell from years of unaired sweat and smoke and perfume; it's worse in the dressing room where sweaty high-heels ferment behind lockers night after night.

Natalie shimmies into a tasseled two-piece and straps on a pair of high-heeled spikes, smudges fat black lines around her eyes and rubs her mother's red lips together. She twists a strand of black hair around her finger. It reaches almost to her waist, wavy with reddish tips from an Elsa Brown dye job two years ago. She lights a cigarette and watches herself smoke, pretends she's Rita Hayworth, Elizabeth Taylor in garters from *Cat on a Hot Tin Roof*. Fuck Elsa Brown. Fuck Miss America.

The music fades, replaced by clapping. She's up. A dancer with a yellow costume and an armful of bills charges through the beaded divider, red-faced and panting. "Thank you, Dawne," the DJ says. "Now let's all give a warm welcome to another Sugar Lovely, *Natalie*."

The initial banging notes of Jimi Hendrix's "Foxy Lady." Natalie positions herself behind the beaded divider, takes two breaths, then saunters through the beads. *You know you are a sweet little...love maker.* The edges of the runway glow with red lights. Lighting in a strip club is part denial and part disguise: black lights, strobe lights, red lights. Particularly the red lights. They soften cellulite and dark circles under eyes and razor burn and bruises and suntan lines and acne; they create the illusion of girls who are soft and creamy and unblemished by reality. *Ooh, Foxy Lady.*

Her coverlet flutters to the ground. The bar patrons clap and hoot as she slinks to the end of the stage, makes a few slow, exaggerated turns, and reaches for the two fingerprint-smeared brass poles. She lets her body fall, looping the pole several times. A balding man in a white button-down shirt stands at the edge holding money; he tucks a bill on either side of her tasseled bottoms.

Center stage she unhooks her bustier, teasing the audience. Her moves are tested, effective, polished. Suggestive without being sleazy. Men holding dollar bills crowd the stage, captivated. Toothy grins. Adoring eyes. The second best part of her job.

Her set finishes. The stairwell leading from backstage to the bar is covered with lipstick-kiss marks—the carved initials of a thousand women who have passed through these doors. She presses her lips to the dingy wall and her fresh red kiss stays behind.

III

"Your father likes a lot of makeup," my mother says, sliding into a pair of white satin pants.

I sift through the bowl of trial-sized Avon lipsticks. They have perfect names like Terra Cotta Sunset or Boysenberry Freeze. Apricot Blush. Cocoa. Scarlett. Wine. Desert Sun. Mocha # 17.

The bathroom counter is covered with an assortment of tubes and bottles and jars and hot rollers. I know the routine: First the corrector stick under her eyes like baseball players but white instead of black. Then the liquid foundation—tap, tap, tap over everything and smoothed in with a squishy, triangle-shaped sponge that I press between my fingers like a little triangle marshmallow. Her face is a shiny tan mask. Now soft powder with a big, poofy brush. I love the way the bristles feel against my cheek, dust hanging in the air.

I open and close all the tiny tubes of Avon tester-sized lipsticks while she puts on eyeshadow: Turquoise Sky and Misty Meadow. Black eyeliner and Blackest Black mascara. I hand her the well-worn palette of rouge—her favorite color has since become discontinued so she savors every last grain—she sweeps peachy blush on her cheekbones, dusts her chin and forehead. And then the grand finale: lipstick. She always wimps out when it comes to the lipstick. I will always wear red.

"It's because I'm a spring," my mother says, outlining her lips with Frosted Peach. "My coloring looks best in pinks and pastels. You're a winter, so you can wear red and black and royal blue and emerald green."

Now the lesson moves to the bed and her open jewelry boxes. I take out each piece while she unrolls her curlers and releases big, honey-colored ringlets. My favorite necklace is a chunky medallion with blue and coral stones.

"Why don't you ever wear this one?"

"Costume jewelry," she says, as if that were bad and as if I, by liking it, had poor taste. By now her hair is swept into big honey-colored waves. She sits with me briefly to pick out earrings. I offer my favorites, two long rhinestone teardrops that look like the crown jewels of England, but she says those are too heavy. I add bracelets to my thin wrists as she tortures herself into support hose that give her vinyl, mannequin legs. She powders her underarms and sprays herself with White Shoulders before sliding into a white sequined tube top.

She's like a big, glowing angel that I can hardly see through my gathering tears.

"What's the matter?" she asks, turning away from the mirror.

"I'm never going to be as beautiful as you."

She sits next to me and squeezes my bony shoulders. "You're not insecure, are you?"

"What does that mean?"

"You think no one loves you."

"No, I know you love me," I lie.

It's Halloween. I'm Miss America. My mother wrote the words "Miss America" in black marker on a sash of burlap. I'm wearing all the jewelry I want from my mother's jewelry box, even her rhinestone dangling earrings. It's the first time I've been allowed to wear dangling earrings. And red lipstick. I have a rhinestone necklace tied into my hair as my crown. My father and his co-worker are taking me door to door. They're both smiling at me in a way that I don't understand.

"Will you marry me in about ten years?" the friend of my father says to me. I blush. "When she's older you're gonna have your hands full," he says to my father.

They both snicker.

"Why are you ignoring those guys, Mom?"

I'm talking about those guys at the stoplight next to us, the ones waving and whistling at her. She just looks straight ahead as if she doesn't see them.

"They think you're pretty."

My mother doesn't say anything. One blows her a kiss. I don't understand. Doesn't every woman want men to whistle and blow kisses? I know I do.

The light turns green. We start driving. If men honk their horn and whistle at me when I get older, *dear god please let that happen,* I swear I'll be more appreciative.

IV

Stripper Tip #1: By becoming friends with the cocktail waitresses, you can bribe them to mark off several drinks on your drink sale quota each night.

Stripper Tip #2: If a customer doesn't tip you in addition to buying you a drink, drink it fast and leave the table.

Stripper Tip #3: If you change costumes between every set, you can legitimately kill lots of time in the dressing room. If you're working a day shift, you can even read a book in the back and no one will notice.

Stripper Tip #4: Never leave your drink unattended with a customer, or else the customer is going to be tempted to see if that Fuzzy Navel he just paid $10 for actually has any "Fuzzy" in it.

Stripper Tip #5: Costumes that glow under black lights make you look thinner.

Stripper Tip #6: Underarm deodorant glows under black lights.

Stripper Tip #7: Frosted lipstick doesn't show up on stage.

Stripper Tip #8: Sparkle gel in cleavage makes you look sweaty.

The club is crowded for a Thursday. Natalie's not in the mood to sit and chat with customers. She requests "anything rock and roll" for her next set and sneaks back to the dressing room before the staff catches her. Too late. She's been spotted. She acquiesces, steering into the closest swivel chair as if that's where she was headed all along and wonders to herself: Would you like it better if this man, this chemistry professor with the Russian accent who always smells of lavender soap, pulled out a $100 bill—would that make it more interesting for you to sit here and smile and lie about the details of your life? Would it change the fact that you know he's handcuffed himself under the table in order to play out his dominatrix fantasy in a socially acceptable way, that he'll expect you to retrieve his wallet from his coat pocket and pay for all the drinks with his money? Does he suspect that you're drinking $10 glasses of orange juice, that the shot you ordered for yourself is just water? Does he know and just not care, and if you were to yell, "Butt out and buy me a drink, bitch," would he find this secretly exciting and tip you extra when he finally uncuffs himself to drive home? Well, you say, how's your week been, as if this overweight man with flared, slightly pointed nostrils isn't handcuffed, and you talk about things, boring things, what books you're reading and what movies you've seen. You always attract the professors and the intellectuals, you're too All-American to be nasty, there's too much Elsa Brown Modeling School running through your veins. The television anchormen still wearing their suits, the visiting celebrities–that's how you met Sean Penn and the Superstars of Wrestling. Jake the Snake autographed one of the dancer's asses but you're not like that, you're the one who makes people snicker when you cuss–and would you be happier if he gave you $20 bills rather than $5 at a time so you could hurry up and be done with it? Well, you say again, drink gone, shot of water followed by lime, I'm up again soon so I should go get ready, and you tip yourself $40 from his wallet as he watches because, really, what is he going to do about it, and you walk up the stairs, two drinks marked off your nightly bar quota and another hour of your life wasted, thrown like pocket change to the sidewalk.

V

"Stay still," my mother says, coming at me with a mascara wand. We're backstage at the Miss Nebraska Pre-Teen Pageant, 1985. I'm twelve years old. She lathers turquoise eye shadow on my eyelids, the way she wears it. It matches my gown. This is my first pageant, and I'm a head taller than most of the other girls. Next year I'll be too old for Miss Nebraska Pre-Teen.

Pageants are a big deal in my family. Some people watch the Super Bowl; we watch pageants. We make popcorn. We make scorecards out of yellow legal paper. As the contestants are introduced, my father points out the women who have "eagle beaks," "giraffe necks," or "hair that looks like it's hiding a country ham." He likes the ones with Priscilla Presley eye makeup.

I always get to stay up late to see the five finalists squished into the soundproof glass box with their big smiles, the excitement as they are eliminated one by one. And then the sparkling crown, bestowed by the reigning queen on her crying replacement.

So when I came home from school four months ago and found the pamphlet waiting for me on the dining room table, I knew it was an omen: The Miss Pre-Teen Pageant, for girls ages eight to twelve.

I spent every Saturday going door to door, raising sponsorship for my entry fee. I spent evenings tottering around in my mother's high heels with a book on my head. I practiced "Cripple Creek" every day on my banjo. And I just spent the last two days learning dance routines, taking group pictures and doing preliminary interviews.

My father sticks his head in the door of the dressing room. "We're going to be late," he says with that stern look that's supposed to remind me that even in front of all these other girls he will still spank me if he has to. "Let's go."

But then he takes my arm, so proud. I've never seen my father so proud. He's even wearing the three-piece caramel-colored suit with the white, ruffly shirt and shiny tan shoes that he bought for Uncle Mark's wedding. His hair is freshly dyed.

We wait in line with dozens of other girls in frilly gowns, some with their fathers, some with older brothers. One girl's escort is in full military dress—I can tell my father wishes he would have thought of that. One poor girl is being escorted by her mom.

When it's my turn I have perfect posture. Peacock-blue eyelids. I walk center stage towards the judges, do a slow turn, and return to my father's arm. I hear my name and soft clapping from the audience.

Eventually all the girls are gathered on the stage. I'm glad I'm tall; there are dozens of us. The final names are called, "Fourth runner up..."

One of the blond, curly girls steps forward, crying as they hand her roses.

"The third runner up is..." She calls my name.

Me? I step forward and burst into tears as someone hands me a bunch of red roses and an enormous trophy.

The trophy is so big it hardly fits on my bookshelf. It doesn't say my name, though. Just "Miss Nebraska Pre-Teen: Third Runner Up."

Stripper Tip #9: Never loan money to another dancer.

Stripper Tip #10: Always carry a razor and shaving cream.

Stripper Tip #11: Smoking pot in the bathroom only makes the night drag on forever.

Stripper Tip #12: Always choose your own music, even if your constant requests annoy the DJ. Tipping him helps. There is nothing worse than having to dance to eleven minutes of Meatloaf.

Maybe this is a bad idea, you think. You're not eighteen anymore, or sixteen. You're thirty-five years old, mother of two children, respectable wife of a research scientist. You have a Masters degree.

You're already imagining what waits for you as you drive toward the Sugar Lounge. You've been replaying this scene in your mind so many times it's as if it's already happened. The bouncer stands under the awning, guarding the door with quiet intimidation. He looks exactly the same except for a cap of gray hair. Joe, right? He nods. I'm sure you don't remember me, but I used to work here a really long time ago. My name was Natalie. You wait for recognition. He studies your face. Begins to nod slowly.

I remember you, Natalie, he says, raising one eyebrow. You worked here a long *long* time ago.

Downtown Omaha, Old Market, Howard Street. You already know it doesn't exist anymore, because you called for their hours and got an automated disconnect notice, but you want to go stand in front of the building, at least. You want to stand in front and see what happens to you.

You plug the meter and walk down the street and see the wig shop has become a Cajun restaurant and the S & M shop has become a sushi bar and you calculate how many more sushi bars will have to move in before the whole place loses its charm, and then you ask yourself: is it really hipper here or is everyone just younger?

Around the corner. Everything is melting into place. Was it always two stories? It must have been, the dressing room was always upstairs. The sign says Alley Katz with the outline of a saxophone player against a city skyline. The parking lot has expanded. It seems so small from the outside—tiny, even. Like a little brick closet. How did we all fit in there?

The door to Alley Katz is open. Of course you go in. Right away you recognize the feeling of the room, even though it's been painted blue and the stage is pushed all the way against the wall. An old guy sits at the bar eating something long and messy.

"Is this your place?"

He wipes his mouth and half stands. "Yep. What can I do for you?"

"Did this place used to be a strip club?"

"Yep, five, six years ago. I've had this place for three years. Ralph still owns the building. You know Ralph, the owner?"

"Yeah. He's still around, huh?"

"Yep, he's got a new club off the highway, the Love Shack. It's all nude."

"Right off the highway?"

"Yep."

"I think I might have passed it driving up here."

"Yeah, that's it."

"Maybe I'll go say hi. I was just wondering what happened to everyone."

"Don't tell me you used to be a dancer."

So many things you can say at this moment. It's important to say the right one. "What if I told you I was?"

"I would say good for you," he says.

You ask to use the bathroom but once in the hallway you climb the first few steps to the dressing room instead. Your lipstick mark is faded, a red graffiti kiss. After all these years they've never painted over them.

VI

The cab drops Natalie at Dick's Yum Yum club, duffel bag in hand. *God, one more night of this and I'm going to shoot myself*, she thinks. *And no, it's not because I'm being pimped out on the side or dodging my lecherous boss or hooked on heroin. I'm not making $1,000 a night, I'm not snorting cocaine off the bar, and nobody is stalking me. Just because I work in a strip club does not make me an idiot.*

Dick's Yum Yum Club is in Council Bluffs, across the Missouri River from Omaha. Dick, the owner, is a short man ala Danny Devito, but it's his business partner, Diane, that generates all the gossip. Although Diane is married to one of the bartenders, she's always looking for girls to go in the limo and see if "we can still give old Dick a rise." New dancers are warned immediately.

Natalie's been working here for months but she's never really paid much attention to Suzi Cooper. Maybe it's that big hair. Big, big hair that she wears in an oversized banana clip like a frizzy horse's mane. Trailer trash.

Natalie doesn't care at all about Suzi until now, when she overhears Suzi telling a customer that last night she was "naked in the hot tub with Anna."

With the exception of gross Diane, Natalie's under the impression that dancers shouldn't be attracted to other dancers. It just doesn't happen, or at least it doesn't happen openly. But it happens in porn, and Natalie knows all about porn. She learned everything she knows about sex from her father's secret stash. So she knows that it *does* happen. Like a flap barely lifted on a secret, the promise of something velvet and golden just beyond, Suzi's comment has opened a door.

Maybe Suzi was plotting even then. Maybe Natalie sits a little closer, maybe makes a strategic comment or two. Maybe she flagrantly digs. Maybe she asks Suzi if Anna is her girlfriend. Maybe Suzi says, "I'm not a dyke" and rolls her eyes as she leaves. That's Suzi's style.

But the seed has been planted. Natalie watches Suzi dance against a set of poles: she's petite, with strong thighs and a muscular, flat chest and the longest, straightest nipples Natalie has ever seen. But what she notices now are Suzi's full lips, the way her eyes twinkle when she smiles, the slight gap between her front teeth. "It's lucky," Suzi says. "It means I'm going to be rich."

Natalie has watched a lot of women on stages, on runways, but not with real appreciation. Not like this. She mentions it to her boyfriend that night in bed. He says exactly what she expects him to say:

Can I join in?

When I was fourteen my father gave me the accumulation of his life's wisdom: If you want to keep a man, learn to swallow.

This was several years after they had started having "slumber parties" with our next-door neighbors where they all wore matching pajamas. Some weekends we'd alternate and all sleep at the neighbor's house, me alone in the guest bedroom and the four of them in the king-sized master bed, Bob and Carol and Ted and Alice style.

The slumber parties were only the latest in a string of similar events. Like the way my father dressed my mother up in wooden heels and no bra and paraded her around the mall, following ten paces behind. Or our series of pretty college babysitters. Or the bachelors and newlywed couples that always seemed to come to dinner.

My mother was a pageant girl herself, always beautifully posed in those old black-and-white group shots of all the contestants in their '60s coifs and A-line satin gowns. But my mother never won a pageant. Even in the photographs her eyes are shy, embarrassed by all the attention. The other girls cheated, she claimed. It was all a popularity contest.

She would blame the hairdresser, the too-tight shoes, the fact she had been crying all night with nerves.

My father loved to tell stories about my mother's loser, outcast boyfriends; he taunted her about her morning breath, stinky feet, beak nose, giraffe neck, her one slightly discolored tooth from an old root canal. As I approached puberty, I got it too: my budding breasts were mosquito bites, ironing boards. When guests were over he hung up my training bra with a note that said "feed me."

Right about the time I discovered my father's vast porn collection, my mother discovered Jesus and the slumber parties stopped. So my father's affair began. Every evening for five years he ate dinner, showered, shaved, put on clean clothes and went "next door." If we needed him in the evenings we'd have to call next door. If I wanted to spend quality time with him it had to be while he was shaving.

"She" became a loaded word. Fights were intense and unpredictable. I stopped bringing friends home. My mother destroyed gifts, gave away any clothing reminiscent of "her" or their slumber parties. I was endlessly grounded, chained to the house.

Then one night I was home alone. Fed up, I had a bottle of aspirin and a Capri Sun. I dumped out the pile of little white discs and counted: fifty-two.

I heard twenty aspirin would kill you, so I took twenty. Then I took the rest, very fast. I lay on the carpet and waited for the Angel of Death to come and carry me away, but after an hour I was still waiting. Poison was singing about every rose having its thorn. The death part must take a while, I decided, so I did what any fifteen-year-old would do: I snuck out.

I hurried to a party that I wasn't allowed to attend—I *was* grounded, after all. But I was going to die soon, so what did it matter? I don't remember the details of the party, and once there, the aspirin dissolving in my stomach seemed as surreal as the Cheetos or the vodka-grape soda mixture in my plastic cup. After an hour or so, I began to dread the severe punishment that was surely awaiting me at home when I was discovered missing.

I stumbled home, past the huge dark lumps of suburban houses and the sounds of sputtering sprinklers, and my mind vacillated between the excuse I would use to explain why I had gone to a forbidden party and the excuse I would use to explain why I was going to die. I was woozy. I imagined myself falling dramatically through my front door, on the verge of death, and my father taking me in his arms and weeping, "No!"

My father sat in his bathrobe in front of the TV, the couch already made up with blankets and pillows from previous weeks.

"Where have you been?" he said without looking at me. "You're grounded for another month."

Dying now seemed like a very bad idea. I ran upstairs to the bathroom and tried to puke. I watched the room spin, pleading, *I made a mistake. I don't want to die any more.*

I begged and bargained until sleep finally won and the next morning I woke up alive.

My parents found out about the whole ordeal three weeks later when the only friend I'd confided in told our high school principal, Father Frank Dimitri, "for my own protection." What a load of crap. I should have kept my mouth shut. My parents were waiting for me after school with torches lit, lynching rope ready. My father held photocopied sheets of my diary; my mother slowly explained how they would never be able to leave me alone in the house because I might clean out the medicine cabinet like some common druggie. That same day they packed my bag and drove me to Lutheran Hospital, checked me into the teen psychiatric ward, told the nurses that I was to have no visitors, and left me to watch the holiday lights go up, and then come down, outside my seventh-story window.

My parents split six months after I was released from the hospital—they couldn't stand up to the scrutiny that followed a daughter's suicide attempt. The precarious marriage was finally put out of its misery and my father moved out, leaving only a note on my bed saying I hadn't been much of a daughter.

Even now I still think about his strange, almost prophetic advice: If you want to keep a man, learn to swallow. I've swallowed so much, Dad, I want to say. More than you ever told me I would have to.

VII

Today is the day! Today we'll finally be getting our Elsa Brown Modeling School makeup! I've been waiting forever for this day, for the Elsa Brown lipsticks, eyeshadows, lip brushes, blushes, face washes, toners and the all-important Vitamin E stick. Not just any girl can have Elsa Brown makeup. It's only for models. You can't just walk into Walgreens and buy it.

I've dreamed of this day ever since I saw Vanessa Worley's pure Vitamin E stick with "Elsa Brown Modeling School" in gold letters in fifth-period Spanish class. She had something we all wanted and she knew it, applying it over and over to her already glossy lips.

Now in my spare time I study magazines: poses, fashion trends, hairstyles, accessories, makeup tips. Sometimes I linger on a beautiful face that's different from mine, a blue-eyed beauty or the Noxema girl with the red spiral curls. I'm stuck with dark hair, dark eyes, dark skin. My mother insists that she always wanted to have brown hair and brown eyes, but I know she's lying.

I'm paying for modeling school myself from my part-time job at Burger King. Every penny is bringing me closer to the runways in Milan and my face on Noxzema ads. And for three hours a week I belong here, in my meticulously planned outfits, in Elsa Brown's studio, with the plush white carpet and the fresh flowers in clean bowls. Black and white composite cards line the mirrored walls, telling the stories of girls who have come before me.

A typical day in modeling school goes like this: First we do outfit critiques. We stand on a wooden stage and the others discuss: Is this outfit flattering to her shape? Do the colors work for her skin tone? How about her makeup? Is she over or under accessorized? What about her shoes?

Outfit critiquing is followed by my least favorite part of

class: current events.

After outfits and current events, we address the particular business of the day: diet, hairstyles, makeup, skin care, nail care. One week we learned how to model at tea rooms. Another week we learned runway turns. This week we're learning makeup. Next week is hair and in two weeks we'll do preliminary photo shoots.

My modeling instructor is six feet tall and always carries a gallon jug of water, "hydrating herself" regularly. The makeup guy is impossibly gay and calls everyone "gorgeous." Whenever Elsa Brown makes a cameo appearance it's as if CoCo Chanel herself has teleported into our midst. Together they've infected our class with a desire for "it"— we've started chopping off our hair like Linda Evangelista and wearing higher and higher heels. And after today I'll be able to whip out my own Elsa Brown Vitamin E stick in Spanish class, envied by all.

They hand out the brown tackle boxes filled with bottles and tubes and brushes and mirrors and tweezers. Screw prom, by the way. I'm not surprised no one asked me. All the boys are immature, whispering about me whenever I walk by. I don't care. Vanessa Worley just got a modeling contract in New York. She's going somewhere. I'm following.

Dance Move #1: Downward Facing Deer. With your back to the audience, grab two poles and stand with your legs apart. Jiggle your butt as you lower your torso to the ground. While you are down between your legs, put your finger in your mouth. Then pop up quickly and let your hair fan through the air.

Dance Move #2: Lovebirds. When a customer comes up to the stage with a dollar bill folded lengthwise in his mouth, swivel down until you're in a squat then take the other end of the dollar in your mouth, closer and closer until your noses almost touch and then break away at the last second.

Dance Move #3: The Kan-Kan. Lie on stage, on your back with your legs raised. Now kick one of your legs, then the other, then trace circles in the air like a kan-kan dancer, occasionally spread them in a V and back up. When you are done, roll onto your stomach and up to all fours.

Dance Move #4: Mirror, Mirror on the Wall. Put both your hands on the back mirror and lean against it. Stick your butt out, walking your legs in place so that your butt jiggles from side to side. When finished, back up to the mirror and slowly melt to the floor.

Dance Move #5: The Whispering Kitten. Mouth the lyrics of any song while looking a customer in the eye. My favorites: "Justify My Love" by Madonna or "Get Off" by Prince. Or anything by Sade.

Denny's is slammed. The after-bar crowd, the bartenders and cocktail waitresses and heavy drinkers who are not yet ready to call it a night fill the tables.

"So how do you like working at Dick's?" Suzi asks, lighting a Marlboro 100.

Natalie dumps cream into her coffee. "It's fine."

"Where did you work before?"

"The Sugar Lounge."

Natalie, Suzi and a few other dancers are sitting at a yellow vinyl booth with Channel 7 anchorman Michael Green, his entourage of fans (or maybe they're his cameramen), and his bubble of self-importance. It's three o'clock in the morning and he's still wearing his suit, probably so they'll recognize him. Suzi's laughing at his jokes but Natalie has seen him in the bar plenty of times before and the novelty has worn off. She's only here because Suzi invited her.

"Do you know Lucy?" Michael Green interjects, passing the coffeepot. "I think she used to work at the Sugar Lounge, too."

Of course he'd be a fan of Lucy. Lucy would lift her top and let a customer suck her nipple when the bouncer wasn't looking. "Yeah, I know her."

Natalie attacks a plate of Moons Over My Hammy, starved after dancing all night. She thinks Suzi's been flirting with her these last weeks, but she's not sure. Natalie has barely dated as it is, let alone been a seducer of women. Her total experience with sex is:

1) Christopher Weiss, the junior she picked up at Pizza Hut and promptly seduced once she decided there was no reason to hold onto her virginity.

2) Eli Shumaker, the only boy she dated in high school.

3) Mike Martinez, Eli's best friend.

4) Carey Frost, the pre-med student she met at an after hour's club last year. They're officially engaged, but he goes to college an hour away and only returns to Omaha on the weekends.

5) Jack Leigh, the twenty-six-year-old hairdresser who is her boyfriend during the week when Carey is away. Jack has white blond hair and eyelashes that he dyes black like that guy in *Clockwork Orange*.

But how do you pick up a woman? In the movies there is usually a game of truth or dare, a hot tub, chocolate syrup or whipped cream, cherries, a few men looking on. Maybe she can get Michael Green to start a game of truth or dare? She hasn't been able to get the images out of her mind for the last few weeks, ever since she decided that Suzi was indeed beautiful. Trashy and beautiful.

As Natalie schemes, Michael Green puts his hand on her forearm and leaves it there for a beat too long. Natalie knows he has a wife and kids at home. She rolls her eyes. Asshole.

VIII

I met Levon Brightman at the Sugar Lounge fifteen years ago; he's a photographer. He came in one evening and asked if I'd ever been a model. Of course, I answered. It wouldn't be the first time I fell for that line. He offered me free prints if I ever wanted to model for him. Turns out Levon was legit and often used strippers as models—they weren't shy about taking off their clothes and they were always anxious to see themselves as artsy, black-and-white nudes.

Later, when I moved away from Omaha to go to college and commuted back to the Sugar Lounge on the weekends, I would often stay at Levon's funky Old Market loft. He introduced me to iced coffee and white pizza and took my first professional acting headshots.

I sit in my Old Market hotel room wondering if Levon still lives in Omaha. A quick search through the phone book provides my answer. Will he even remember me? It's been a long time, after all.

"Natalie!" he says when he answers the phone. "Are you in Omaha?"

"I am. I'm just here for a few days. I'm on a sort of fact-finding mission."

"Why don't you meet me at the coffeeshop? Do you remember where my old apartment was?"

"Of course."

"It's just a block from there. I'll meet you in thirty minutes."

My stomach flutters as I take a shower, washing the sweet, smoky smell of the Sugar Lounge-turned-Alley Katz from my hair. If anyone would know what happened to Suzi, Levon might. He was friends with all the girls.

I recognize him immediately. His black frizzy hair has chunks dyed blue and hot pink. I notice the gray in between.

He surprises me by saying that he got married. The surprise is lessened when he reveals his spouse is a man.

"So why do you want to find Suzi so bad?" he asks. "Is this some sordid tale of past love?"

I laugh. "No, not really." I tell him about my dream.

"Fascinating." He takes a sip of his cappuccino and smiles. Levon has a way of smiling that unpeels layers from you. "You're still gorgeous, by the way. You should let me take your picture."

"Oh, I don't know. I've had two kids..."

"You don't have to take your clothes off," he teases. "We can do it right here, under the trees. It's so lovely in the fall." He reaches across the table and holds my chin, turns my head slightly, studying my profile. "You've gotten a few wrinkles."

"I know."

"But they're nice. They work for you. You know I have pictures of Suzi in my studio, don't you?"

"You do?"

"Of course. On print. I have all you Sugar Lounge dancers. I probably have the best documentation of strippers in all of Omaha."

"How long ago did you take them?"

"Oh, years ago. After her boob job."

"I heard it was terrible."

"You can see for yourself. I don't remember you two being such great friends."

"We weren't."

"Just lovers?"

"Not really lovers, either. That sounds too romantic."

"Fuck buddies?"

"Not even that. We only had sex a few times. Mostly she used me."

"Ah," he says, sitting back. "So you want to tell her off?"

"No. I don't know why I want to see her. I wouldn't give her my number if I did find her."

Levon shifts in his chair. He studies my face. "Do you date mostly women?"

"No, men. I've been married twice."

"How've they been?"

"So-so."

"Tragic breakups?"

"No, not really. Just the usual."

"Have you slept with any women since Suzi?"

"A few. Years ago. Nothing meaningful."

"What's 'nothing meaningful'?"

"Mostly threesomes. I slept with a girl a few times after college but she had a boyfriend. Oh, and I picked up a girl at a bar once."

"Gay bar?"

"Straight bar. I slept with her and never called her again."

"You're such a dog. And how about men?"

"Well, men are easier. I know what's expected."

He drops his voice. "You secretly want to sleep with Suzi again?"

I drop my voice to match. "I don't think so. Besides, she's probably riddled with diseases."

Levon raises his eyebrows like he doesn't believe me.

"I don't."

"I heard from Celeste a few months back..."

I blush.

"I still have those pictures. They're beautiful," he says.

"I'm not sure I want to see them."

"Why didn't you have sex with her?"

"She had a boyfriend, remember?"

"Maybe your dream is telling you to embrace your inner lesbian."

I shake my head slowly. "I don't think that's why I'm here."

Levon and I spiral up the stairs, the stairwell covered in graffiti from the many artists squatting in the building. "It's the same building but I've changed apartments," he says, unlocking a door.

It's a pea-green loft with tall windows covered by fire escapes. Black and white nudes cover every wall. Levon digs through envelopes and starts spreading photos on the couch.

"God, it's been forever since I've gone through the old prints. All my photos are digital now. Here's JJ, remember her?" Of course I remember JJ: tiny, Asian, aerobics instructor, contortionist. She had perfect black shiny hair. She was always laughing, always joking. In the photo she lays on the floor with a piece of gauze over her lower body, looking out a window. Four squares of light from the window rest across the contours of her face.

"It's beautiful."

"Oh, here's Alice," he says, handing me a photo. "You'll like this one." She's naked and wrapped in a snake.

"And here's Hope," he says, piling pictures on my lap.

"Wow, I forgot about her." Hope the Cokehead. She was a great dancer—I stole a lot of her moves. I remember the day she stopped by work to pick up her check and her kid was with her. She had her hand over his eyes the whole time.

"I'm still looking for Suzi," he says. "Ah, here's Carey's wedding."

"You photographed Carey's wedding?"

"Yeah. He married some blond girl. She wasn't nearly as pretty as you." He hands me a proof sheet with rows of thumbnail photos.

Carey, my first fiancé, the med student I cheated on for years. I recognize his best man, his family. "He looks happy," I say. "Do you keep in touch with him?"

"Some. He's a doctor now. Lives in Michigan I think. Remember the pictures you two took together?" He hands me another sheet: Carey and I naked and wet, climbing a rope. I remember that day, it took us forever to secure the rope from one of the tall rafters in the loft and adjust the curtains right. I remember swinging through the air; we were trying to hold onto the rope and each other without falling. Those pictures were featured in an exhibit. I have copies of them in my trunk at home.

"Or how about these?" he says, handing me photos of myself, my hair in varying lengths. "I used this one in a show," he says, pointing to a close-up of me with long fake lashes. "I'm looking for the ones of you and Celeste, too, but I can't find them. Oh, here's Suzi."

My heart jumps. There she is. I immediately look at her boob job. Well, it's not as bad as I imagined. She's wearing her hair the way she always did, in a banana clip so that the remainder cascades down her back in her signature horse's mane. "She looks the same as I remember," I say. "When did you take these?"

He looks over my shoulder, points to the date penciled at the bottom. "Says nineteen-ninety-six."

"I'd been gone for three, maybe four years by then."

"I really haven't seen her since. Last thing I heard she was dating some bar owner, but even if it was true you know what the turnover is like in those places."

I scrutinize her face in one of the close-ups. It's been years since I've looked into Suzi's face. She's smiling mischievously, light glinting from her dark eyes. Her curly hair casts curly shadows on her cheek. She's trying to be sexy and at the same time I can tell she's putting on an act. That's always how it was with her.

"Oh, here's you and Celeste," he says. I almost don't want to look at the impromptu photo shoot following a late-night breakfast at the Leavenworth Café, how Levon dared us to kiss and let him take pictures.

After a peek they're not nearly as raunchy as I remember. They're even kind of pretty. Celeste's face is contorted in mid-kiss, coming at me. My face is half hidden by long hair. I mean hell, it was the early '90s, girls kissing girls was a novelty. But the picture makes me feel nervous.

The first time I slept with Suzi and Jack the Hairdresser we were at Suzi's apartment after work (later I found out that it wasn't Suzi's apartment at all). Even though Jack was technically my boyfriend, I was willing to sacrifice our relationship for the greater good of my sexual education. We ordered pizza, played a little truth or dare, then Suzi put on some porn.

We sat girl-boy-girl on the love seat. Ten seconds into the porn Suzi started kissing Jack then reached for me. She smelled like the bar but her mouth and skin and tongue were softer than any I had ever kissed. Soon she was tugging our clothes off. Her shoulders still sparkled from glitter gel. We were naked. The doorbell rang. Domino's Pizza. Oh shit. That deep dish pepperoni had sounded so good thirty minutes earlier; the pizza boy kept blushing and looking away as Jack searched his pants pockets for money—maybe he thought we'd invite him in. We didn't.

Once he was gone we abandoned the pizza. Mostly what I remember from that night is the feeling of Suzi's wild, curly hair brushing the insides of my thighs.

IX

Stripper Tip #14: Never put it past any dancer to steal your sweaty, stinky costume out of your duffel bag when you are on stage.

Stripper Tip #15: If a group of men comes in wearing business suits and says they're from out of town, do not decide to speak with a British accent for the rest of the evening, because guaranteed one of them will be back the next night and you'll give yourself away.

Stripper Tip #16: When your best friend from high school comes into the club to see what you've been up to, there is really no need to be embarrassed, because, you never know, she could be in a borrowed costume within an hour, crawling on the floor of the main stage (*nobody* expected that one).

My husband says I have "sexual issues." "You need to see a therapist," he said to me before I left. "I'm a man and I have needs. You're just playing some kind of game with me."

"I'm not," I said. "I'm just confused."

"And what am I supposed to do? Just wait around while you decide if you ever want to have sex again? I'm not your father."

"I know."

"I don't think you do. You're just running away from your patterns."

Ah, my patterns. They always like me at first. They tell me how wonderful I am (or beautiful or smart or a goddess), so then I like them back. That's all it takes. Sex will start out hot and heavy and fizzle within a year, after I get tired of putting on the bells and whistles. Almost all the breakups are initiated by me. As soon as my spell appears to be wearing off and they're no longer enamored by me I move on quickly, before I can be discarded. Once my mind is made up I rarely look back.

There was Michael, Jason, Kelly, Charlie, Zoe, and some guy at a party whose name I can't remember. Then Guy, the first person who ever said he liked me better without makeup. Then I moved to Maryland, where I slept with and/or dated: Steve, Seth, Bobby, Jesse, and Chad. I slept with Ethan while I was hitchhiking to Missouri and once in St. Louis I dated Ray, a social worker who introduced me to the novel idea that a successful relationship might take work. We broke up. I went back on the road and slept with Kate and then Alex, my first husband. I had an affair with Matthew, got divorced, dated Kevin, Craig and then Ian, my second husband. He told me I was beautiful and three months later I told him I was in love with him and now we're married. As usual, our sex was good at the beginning, if a little insistent. Then needy. Then demanding. When I stopped wanting it he became angry. I've been someone's aspirin my whole life. So I know what comes next. It's what always comes next. That's why I left.

X

I'm ready to go to Dick's Yum-Yum Club. I drive into Council Bluffs and get completely lost and discover that Council Bluffs has a downtown, a real downtown, a little Main Street with yarn stores and a fountain where children play.

I get so turned around I have to finally stop at a gas station and ask for the phonebook: Dick's Yum Yum Club, there it is, Broadway, I knew it was the main drag. I'm nearly fifty blocks away, driving between the deluges of discount grocery stores and fast food stores and automotive stores, splotches of yellow and red and white and black. I remember the building as black but it's actually white with red mudflap girl cutouts nailed to the siding. Dick's Yum Yum Club and Open Everyday and Open at 4. I park the minivan. The asphalt smells fresh, like Disneyworld.

Several men are smoking outside. A new purple awning frames the door above a ribbon of worn red carpet like a landing strip. A bouncer with a baseball hat and a goatee sits on a three-legged stool under the spotlights.

"Do Dick and Diane still own this place?"

"Dick died eight years ago," he says. "Diane'll be in later tonight. Ten dollars." That's new. I dig for ten bucks and he says, "I'll need to see your ID." That's new, too. Then he opens the black padded door with the round portal window and the music assaults me.

I'm Slim Shady yes I'm the real Shady...

The door closes and I'm bathed in a pink glow from all the red light bulbs. I instantly want to smoke a cigarette. The dancer on the corner stage has blunt-cut bangs, black glasses and a black lacy negligee. The smells are familiar, that mixture of cigarettes and perfume, designer fragrances with slogans like "If you like Giorgio, you'll love EXCITE." I can taste the warm, salty cashews from those nut dispensers. I can taste the watery orange juice with square ice cubes.

Past the line of stools at the bar, I'm attracting a few stares. Past the main stage. The carpet is dark enough to trip on except for the glowing multicolored squiggles like the carpeting in Las Vegas hotels. The bartender looks like the lead singer of The Cars, longish hair with over-emphasized ears. The dancer on the main stage is dark-skinned and topless. Everything is exactly as I remember it, all the way down to the portable screen still playing porn and the plush chairs in faded dusty rose. Two more unfamiliar girls on stage—now I'm hurrying through the swinging doors, down a hall that seems dingier and shorter, and into the bathroom. Same orange floors, same two toilets. I go straight into a stall and proceed to hyperventilate.

After many moments I inch from the stall to the sink to the mirror. I try to remember *that* Natalie: red lips, black-lined eyes, wavy black hair. That face is so different from the one looking at me now, the one without make-up, short black hair highlighted by a few bold grays. I dig in my purse for lipstick.

Back in the bar the walls are mirrored so even the customers are forced to look at themselves. I order a whiskey from the bar and slip into the table farthest from the door, next to the cigarette machine. I retrieve eight (*eight!*) dollars and buy a pack of Marlboro 100s and light the first cigarette I've had in five years. Three puffs later I'm dizzy, but smoking in here feels right, just like it used to. Maybe it gave me something to do with my hands. Maybe it had been a way to pass the time between sets. I try to remember how long I worked here and realize I have absolutely no sense of chronology. At some point Suzi and I left together for Red Umbrella, but I couldn't say when or even what season we were in.

Other customers are looking at me with curiosity. I feel conspicuous. I remember the few times an outside woman came into the club, always with a boyfriend, probably on the boyfriend's suggestion to "spice up the sex life." And even if she was trying to downplay it, the jealousy would steam from her pores, poisoning the entire area, and no dancer could come near without inhaling the fumes.

"You can't smoke in here," the cocktail waitress says, bringing my drink. "Smoking ban's been in effect since July."

Sorry. I put it out. The new girl on my stage is peeling away a long gown, her hair is pinned up and she's wearing white gloves up to the elbow. She catches my eye and smiles friendly, welcoming. I relax. Another dancer walks by wearing a red tube dress. She smiles at me, too. I remember smiling like that, with no reservations. It's not something strangers usually do outside of here.

"Does your sister work here?" This from the man sitting at the table next to me.

I don't want to talk so I just shake my head.

He turns away, but a few minutes later he holds out a rose he's made from a cocktail napkin, a bar trick I've seen a hundred times. "For you," he says. "Smell it." I lift the paper rose to my nose—it smells like rose oil. Does he really carry around rose oil for these occasions? I smile, say thank you. I know he's looking for conversation and I'm an easy target, an anomaly with my little drink, trying to blend into the porn. Most men I met at the club were lonely as hell. For the price of a few drinks an attractive woman would talk to them.

Rose Man approaches the stage with another napkin rose, a dollar bill wrapped around the stem. The dancer is Latina with golden curls, long legs and a white costume. He gives her the rose, the dollar. She smiles the signature smile, kisses him on the cheek. When he returns to his chair he's grinning. Even in this darkened place love tries to sprout like spores normally dormant, shrooming pretty, monstrous, and just as quickly disappears.

An older woman comes through the door, the only other woman in here besides me and the cocktail waitress with her clothes on. She sits at the bar like she's done it a thousand times. Diane? She glances around. Orders something. Wow. It really *is* Diane.

I take my whiskey to the bar and stand beside her. "You're Diane, right?"

"Do I know you?" Her voice is gravely, lips lined with cigarette-smoking hackmarks. Her hair is frosted, swooped away from her face.

"I used to work here a long time ago. I'm Natalie."

"I'm sorry, honey," she says, patting my arm. "I've met too many girls to keep track of them all."

"Do you remember a dancer named Suzi Cooper?"

"No, honey. Sorry."

"Oh."

"I'll buy you a drink though," Diane says, "since you say you worked here."

"Thanks. I heard about Dick."

Diane's face drops. "Yeah, poor Dick. Testicular cancer. He used to say, 'It's got me by the balls now.'"

"I'm sorry."

"Yeah, we were all sorry." She sighs. But she shakes it away and pats me on the thigh. "So, Natalie, how long ago did you work here?"

"It was probably in ninety-one, maybe ninety-two."

"No wonder I don't remember you." She takes a drink from her champagne and watches my face. "So, how did everything turn out?"

"Everything?"

"Your life."

"Oh," I blush, "well, I went to college, bought a van, drove around the country—"

"I did that when I was your age," she says. "You still dancing?"

"I did for awhile. I danced in San Antonio at this really fancy club."

"Never been there," she says. "But I hear those clubs in Texas are something else." She turns to the bartender. "Didn't Destiny go to Texas?"

The bartender shrugs.

"I think she went to Dallas or Houston, I can't remember," Diane says. "So you live in Texas now?"

"St. Louis. I have kids." I dig out two pictures and let Diane and the bartender coo over my sons.

"Where are your kids now?"

"In Kansas City, with my mother."

"And their father?"

"He's in St. Louis. We're married."

"Oh," she says. But she isn't listening to me anymore; she's watching one of the dancers, watching the customers, straightening the stack of coasters at the end of the bar.

"Well, dear, thanks for visiting," Diane picks up her champagne and pats me on the thigh again, like I'm a little kid. "You'll excuse me, I have to do some paperwork in the office."

I'm left with the bartender. He wipes the counter in front of me. "I remember when the stage went all the way to the wall," I say.

"You *did* work here a long time ago. That was even before my time."

"What happened?"

"A truck hit the building from the outside, caved in half the wall."

"Shit. Did anyone get hurt?"

"Nah."

We both let the conversation fizzle as the music ends; a dancer comes off the stage and a new one replaces her. "How about you, you want to get up there and shake it?" The bartender nods to the stage.

I chuckle. "I don't think so."

Stripper Tip #17: If you become convinced to leave work early in order to accompany one of the regulars to a biker party as his date for $300, always get the money upfront. If not you might end up stranded at a trailer park in Council Bluffs with a guy who is too drunk to drive you home, let alone remember that he owes you money.

XI

Practically every girl at the Miss Nebraska Teen Pageant has an Elsa Brown Modeling School tackle box. No matter— only twelve of us are changing into our swimsuits. The girls who didn't make the Top Twelve cut are haunting the edges of the dressing room. Some are trying to be supportive. Some are crying. I only have three minutes to change.

I hate my bathing suit, a peach one-piece with a white bow at my cleavage. When I was trying it on in front of the bathroom mirror last night my mother walked by and said, "Putting on some weight, huh?" and pinched my hips. She's right, peach is a terrible color for me, what was I thinking? I have olive skin, it's going to wash me out, it's not flattering to my hips, but it's too late to get a new one. Instead I paint my lips red and fluff my long hair with squirts of hairspray. My mother is just jealous because she never won a pageant. I'm surprised that she's even here. Ever since I got out of the hospital I've become the black sheep, the whistleblower. It almost makes me miss the screaming.

The Miss Nebraska Teen Pageant is being held at my high school because we have a brand new auditorium. But if the boys at school were afraid of me before, when I was just a model, now they're really scared of me: I was in the loony bin for a month and now I'm a contestant for Miss Nebraska Teen. But if I win, all the shame will be eclipsed by my sparkling crown.

I lift up my boobs and another girl rips off pieces of electrical tape with her teeth and sticks it underneath them like a makeshift bra. It'll hurt to take it off later. The other girls are passing around the sticky spray; when it comes to me I spray both my butt cheeks and then carefully place my bathing suit where I want it to stay. This stuff was made for baseball players to keep their mitts on or something. It feels weird but it works.

With my taped boobs and sticky ass I line up quietly in the darkened wings. I'm number six. We're all checking each other's teeth for lipstick, taking deep breaths. The first girl is called—I'm glad I'm not first. Then the second. Third. When my name is called I suck my stomach in so much I can hardly breathe. Into the bright lights: pause at center stage like we were taught, smile at all the judges scribbling on their score sheets, take my place on the sixth giant oval. The twelve of us will soon be reduced to five.

Backstage all the girls are ripping off their swimsuits and pulling on their evening gowns. Some of their mothers or sisters are helping. I don't need help. My evening gown has a gold lame bust and black velvet to the floor. I got it a year ago to wear to a dance and my mother didn't want to buy me a new one. The mirrors backstage are hot real estate. I add another layer of hairspray to my crunchy hair, put another layer of mascara on eyelashes already stiff. I rub Vaseline on my teeth and admire the way they look without braces.

We return to the stage in the same order. When my name is called I glide into the spotlight, smiling. I try to think about keeping my shoulders back, walking lightly on my heels so I don't sound like a herd of elephants, as my father used to say. Center stage, I turn slowly, showing off the back of my dress. Then glide to my dot. There I remain as the other six follow me, smiling. Smiling. That's another reason not to be first—you have to stand on stage smiling the whole time.

The MC has the envelope. It's time to call the names of the final five. The first girl is called.

The second.

Third.

Fourth.

Fifth.

And I'm still smiling, along with the other girls left behind.

Screw this pageant, I think, keeping my stage face

unchanged until I can go backstage and fall apart. I exit with the other seven losers and hear the crying begin. Tomorrow when I go to class I won't be Miss Teen Nebraska, absolved of sin. And everyone will look at me like I'm still crazy.

XII

A few weeks before my father moved out he was in the den, playing Solitaire on our new computer. This was where you could usually find him, now that the neighbor lady moved away and my mother was in therapy. I was standing next to him, watching him assemble hearts with hearts and clubs with clubs. His head came to my torso. It was our first computer, a clunky, monstrous thing that made squeaks and hisses. He put his arm around my waist, turned his head toward me, pursed his lips, and kissed the end of my breast through my blue and white striped t-shirt.

I couldn't breathe, the wind was knocked out of me. As I slowly backed away, my father looked at me and said, "What, I'm not allowed to kiss your stomach?"

He quietly resumed Solitaire; I ran upstairs to my room, nauseous. My breathing was shallow. The end of my nipple where he had touched me was buzzing and I couldn't scrub it off, couldn't get that feeling to go away.

At the Red Umbrella the bouncer stops me: No unescorted women. What do you mean? No women allowed in unescorted. State Law. Are you meeting someone? No. I used to work here. You used to work here? Yes. When? Seventeen years ago. Are you really not going to let me in because I'm a woman? Isn't that sort of ironic? How do I know you're not a call girl? Huh? Call girls come in here all the time looking for customers. Oh, is that why? Partially. I look at my jean skirt, sandals, navy blue top. I look like I'm going hiking. I gesture to my outfit; do you really think I'm a call girl? That's not the point, ma'am, it's just club policy. Unless you know someone here who can vouch for you. I haven't worked here for seventeen years. I live in St. Louis. I dig through my purse, show him my ID. He's wearing a black suit, black shirt, red tie tucked into one of the holes between the shirt buttons. He stops talking to me and lets in a group of guys. What if I go in with them, then will you let me in? Look, club policy is to say no. I'll vouch for you today but the next time you come in with an escort, okay? Thanks. Twenty dollars. Do you want to check that? He points to my oversized purse. Okay. He takes it and hands me a number. Have fun. He opens the velvet rope and lets me pass.

Metallica is playing as I round the corner. Wow. They remodeled. It used to be one large stage set up high with lots of poles, a brass jungle gym. Now it's a series of round table-stages, chairs gathered around, one dancer per cluster. No poles.

I remember the first night I worked here. I ran into a girl named Bethany that I had known in high school; her braces were off, too. She had the same bleached-out crunchy hair, pasty skin covered by a layer of poorly applied makeup. We'd been friends briefly in ninth grade, when the new freshmen were trying to form alliances. I even spent the night at her house once. She was the first person I knew who took birth control pills; I hadn't even had sex. Now we were colleagues. We sized each other up. I didn't say, "I'm not surprised to see you here. You were always such a slut." She didn't say, "I *am* surprised to see you here. You were always such a priss."

I sit down at a table-stage and a classy cocktail waitress takes my order. The Red Umbrella serves T-bone steaks and baked potatoes. The girls are prettier here, too. They actually clock in. Everywhere else we got an envelope full of cash with our name on it twice a month.

The dancer on the stage in front of me is curvy, with long black hair in big waves. I look around at the dancers on the other stages. They're all wearing gigantic clear plastic platform heels—how do they dance in those things? But they aren't really dancing, the lack of a pole means they just pose, squat, pose, roll around on the stage. The dancer on my stage is crouched away from me. All I can see is a slight strip of blue fabric between her butt cheeks. It's so intimate, more than anything I used to do.

The song ends and the dark-haired girl scoots to the edge of the stage and slowly redresses. Another girl follows her. She has reddish brown hair and a rhinestone choker. She smiles at me and I lay a dollar on the stage and she smiles again, flips over, and gyrates her coochie in my face and receives my dollar with a snap of elastic. She whispers in my ear, "You're beautiful." I blush and she begins to dance again, holding my gaze. I've never been on this side of the stage before. Is this what I used to do? The other men sitting around the stage are smiling private smiles. All of us like little puddles.

I use the bathroom then stop by the bar. "Crown and ginger ale."

"Oh, can I have one, too?"

It's the curvy dancer with long black hair. I'm the customer now. Weird. "And whatever she wants. What do you want?"

"I'll have whatever you're having," she says. *Good answer.* I turn back to the bartender and hold up two fingers.

The bartender nods and leaves.

"I'm Mimi," the dancer says with a hint of a southern accent.

"Nice to meet you." I hold out my hand. Mimi lights a cigarette after squeezing my fingers.

"What, no smoking ban here?"

"We're outside the city limits."

The bartender returns with our drinks and charges me $26. "Mmm, what are we drinking?" Mimi asks as she plunges a straw into the fizz.

"Whiskey." I see the word *yuck* go through her mind as she takes an obligatory swallow and pretends to like it. I used to hate selling drinks. I look at her fake eyelashes, her black party dress, her gold-clasped handbag that she opens to replace the pack. Since I just bought $11 worth of conversation, I motion to her smokes, "Can I have one of those?" The energy between us shifts, like she knows I'm not going to be a big tipper. Mimi lights my slim cigarette and I take a swallow of whiskey. It's strong.

"So, how long have you been a dancer?"

"Oh, about four years." As she talks she touches my shoulder, my arm, my hand resting on the bar. "I worked for a few years when I was twenty-three, then I left for a few years, then came back."

"I used to dance."

The energy between us shifts again to reluctant camaraderie. "Oh, so you know what it's like," she says.

"Yeah. When I was a dancer, women didn't come in the clubs."

"Oh, there are always couples now."

"Couples are a big thing?"

"Oh, yes. I do very well with couples."

I take another drink. "I notice there aren't any poles anymore. How do you dance?"

"You don't really dance."

"Isn't that boring?"

"Totally boring. I work at this other club, The Love Shack, and there they have cages and everything, it's totally retro, you can really shake your butt." The word "butt" sounds funny coming out of her mouth, especially with her little shy southern belle accent, but it doesn't affect me as much as the word "retro." I suppose I'm a relic now.

"Here you can get in trouble for dancing too much," she adds.

"Really?"

"Yep, they come by and tell you to settle down. See, the thing is in this club you don't really have your own personality, they just want you all to be the same girl. They call it classy. But it's boring. If you really want to see some dancing, you should go to the Love Shack. I work there on Wednesdays."

"Ralph owns that place, right? Off the highway?"

"Yeah."

"I used to work for Ralph, too. At the Sugar Lounge. A long time ago."

"You don't look that old."

"I was sixteen."

"Oh," she says, nodding.

"Usually when I tell people I was only sixteen they don't believe me, they say 'how did you...'"

"*You* don't need to know," she finishes for me with a wink. "That goes in the 'You Don't Need to Know' chapter."

I'm laughing. So is she.

"Is Mimi your real name?"

"My real name is Tanya," she says, holding out a hand with French manicured nails.

"My stage name used to be Natalie."

"Natalie," she says, tasting the name. "If my stage name was Natalie I think I'd talk with a Russian accent," and she switches to a European brogue, "I vould say I don't good speak English."

"Where are you from?"

"Where do you think I'm from?" *Another good answer.*

"Georgia?"

"Maryland."

I nod. We toast. She sips again on her barely touched whiskey and grazes my arm. "Well, I have to find out what stage I'm dancing on." Nice exit, I think, one I've used many times myself.

"Nice to meet you." I hold out my hand.

"Nice to meet you."

She touches my hands, shoulders, big fake eyelashes batting. She takes her barely touched drink with her, probably to dump it.

Fourteen years after you've quit dancing, when you find yourself in the middle of a conversation about strippers at a wedding reception, or a book club, or any of the many places that these conversations begin, stay silent. Soon someone will admit they have a friend of a friend who is a stripper and then the inevitable elbow jabbing from the others, "Sure, your *friend* is a stripper," someone will say. To which they will all laugh knowingly, the superior, non-stripper race.

You love being in the middle of these conversations. They never believe *you*, sweet, normal you, was an ex-stripper. So stay silent awhile before dropping the bomb.

"Well my friend told me that she makes a thousand dollars a night."

"Yeah, I heard that, too."

"I knew a girl in college who put herself through medical school as a stripper," (this usually comes from a man). "She worked at night and went to medical school during the day."

"I hear it's dangerous. Stalkers and psychos trying to follow you home every night."

"Oh, it is," another assures. "My friend told me they are *required* to take taxis."

Consensual nods and mock worry. Poor little strippers.

But the mystical, elusive stripper is in their midst and they don't even know it. They sip chai lattes, unaware. Timing is everything. It has to be done in such a way to elicit maximum humiliation—not too early that everyone hasn't revealed their fleshy pink judgmental insides, but not too late that the topic is beginning to wane.

"One of my friends went to The Romper Room and the dancer bent over and a crab jumped into his eye."

"That's disgusting."

"He must be lying."

"No, it's true. He even had to go to the doctor."

The best place to drop the bomb is in a group of women. When it's mixed company you run the risk of impressing the men too much (they'll mentally undress you, place you against an imaginary brass pole to see if the story stands), which will turn the women against you.

"You know, I would do it," one of the women confesses.

"You would?"

"Sure," she says, "if I was getting a thousand dollars a night."

"Well you know, they offer pole dancing classes now at such-and-such yoga studio."

"We should all go." Giggles. Painted fingernails.

The moment to drop the bomb might be passing. If they collectively agree to go to pole dancing classes, then your announcement will only come off as bragging. Or worse—they'll invite you to come along.

"I was a stripper for four years," you say. The women face you, realizing for the first time that indeed you haven't chimed in on this conversation. "Really?" one of them manages amidst much throat clearing and backpedaling through the conversation in everyone's minds: *Did I call them sluts? Whores? Damn. Should have kept my mouth shut.*

This is the golden moment, of course, so let it last. Shrug. "I didn't have to take out any loans for undergrad."

An inaudible sigh—yes, you were one of *those*, the *student* strippers, the "good" ones, studying your textbooks in the dressing room. Thank god, you can hear them thinking. Don't tell them about Suzi or the bachelor parties. "I was sixteen."

Protests crease their foreheads: *Impossible.*

A club would get shut down for that.

The owner would go to jail.

That's what laws are for.

They'll want to call you full of shit but they won't dare. "How did you manage that?" one finally asks.

"I said I was twenty. They never checked my ID. As long as I didn't drink they didn't care."

The women don't like this answer. They fidget. If it's that easy then nobody is safe. "This was in the nineties though. The laws might be stricter now."

Relieved, they all nod—of *course* the laws are stricter now. Whew. What a heathen time that must have been, when sixteen-year-old girls could walk into strip clubs and get jobs and no one was the wiser.

You know the truth, though—why would the laws have gotten stricter? It's not like there's an orange alert crackdown on underage strippers. But at this point they're very uncomfortable so you find a way to let them off the hook, throw in your "official" two cents about the sex industry and then gracefully suggest a new topic of conversation. You have several options. You can go the "Funny, the laws are different in every state" route, or you can go the "Want to hear the weirdest thing that ever happened to me as a stripper" route.

There is a third route, though. You could tell them that, at age sixteen, you felt like you had one-upped society—presented with limitations, told your greatest asset was your looks, you found a way to give yourself financial autonomy and a higher education. That you pat yourself on the back for your clever outsmarting of the society that placed the limitations on you to begin with. Fuck them for their pity. Every stripper you ever met was there on her own accord. There were no pimps waiting in the parking lots. You were more protected dancing on stage than in the real world. At least you chose to be there. At least you got to say yes.

Even now, fourteen years after the day you threw all your costumes in a dumpster, you fantasize about being on those stages again. Never, in any other aspect of your life, have you felt so uninhibited. Even your husband has never seen you like that. Maybe that's why, in your dreams, you're always sneaking to the clubs when he is asleep. And why you were so surprised when he caught up to you.

XIII

When Suzi suggests they rent some movies after work, Natalie doesn't initially realize what kind of movies she means. The XXX Adult Superstore off the highway is full of cars even this late at night.

Inside, Natalie is barely able to concentrate on the multi-flesh-in-various-angles movie jackets, avoiding the solo men shopping in the aisles. Suzi picks out a tape called *Babewatch* and brings it to the counter. Natalie assumes they're going to take it back to her apartment but Suzi nods towards the back of the store. "They have televisions here." She giggles and tickles Natalie into a small plywood room, the size of a closet, with a plywood bench along one side and a television screen suspended from one corner of the ceiling.

They lock the door. The screen sputters to life. The movie is amateur—the filmmaker on the streets of L.A. asking women if they want to come upstairs and masturbate for the camera.

Suzi and Natalie sit on the wooden bench without touching. After twenty minutes Suzi kisses Natalie matter-of-factly, then pulls aside Natalie's shorts and panties. Natalie quickly finds herself pinned between Suzi's head and the images on the screen: a girl being gang-banged by the camera crew, one penis in her vagina, one in her ass, one in her mouth and one in each hand.

"I have to make a phone call," Suzi says when they leave, pulling her blue Trans Am to a drive-up pay phone.

"What? Who are you calling?"

"Eddie."

"At four in the morning?"

"He'll be up." Natalie fidgets while Suzi dials his number, waits. Calls his pager.

"Do you want to come to my house?" Natalie asks when

Suzi finally gives up, and Suzi gives a noncommittal yes. But her pager buzzes a few moments later, and she drops Natalie off at her apartment with a distracted kiss. Later Natalie discovers $20 missing from her wallet, as well as her favorite lipstick.

I'm sixteen years old, standing in the alley behind the Orpheum Theater. It's been over a year since the hospital, nine months since the failed Miss Nebraska Teen Pageant. Inside is the Elsa Brown Modeling School's runway show and graduation. They stopped paying attention to me months ago, but everyone who's paid tuition gets to be in this final runway show. Thrown crumbs. I let them put Zulu knots in my hair, alter my outfits, take pictures. But I know they do it without feeling because I'm never going to be taller than 5'6." Backstage with the others who aren't going anywhere. The short ones, the busty ones practicing their three-point catwalk turns in the green room. But the anorexic girls with boyish thighs are in every sequence. So I know what's coming after this night is over. Nothing.

Two months ago I stuffed my car with everything that would fit and moved into my friend's apartment. It's a one-bedroom, poolside, next to a bar. I slept with the bartender so now I can drink. I telemarket after school then work the graveyard shift at Village Inn until three in the morning, but since I won't ask my parents for money or even consider going back to that fucked-up reality, I have to figure something out. I'm going to graduate from high school early. I talked to the guidance counselor about how: join the Army, get pregnant, or start taking college classes. Maybe I'll sign up for some college classes. I can always drop them later.

Anyway, I'm heading outside to have a cigarette when I hear several of the models talking about dancing. I slow down to listen. What kind of dancing do you do? I finally ask.

"Go-go dancing."

"Really? Do you think they're hiring?"

"They're always hiring," one says. "You should come down. My stage name's Liberty."

Now I smoke in the alley, see the billboard as my dream is dying: Club 22. Beautiful Girls. Open Every Day.

Stripper Tip #18: If, on a slow night, you sit with a strange man you've never seen before and he asks you if you've been saved, don't engage in a conversation. If you do, you might find yourself being saved right in the middle of a strip club in front of the cocktail waitress.

When Suzi moves into Natalie's apartment she brings a bunch of random belongings: marble chess board, giant goulash pot, an assortment of vibrators she lines up in the shower like spent bullet casings. She never quite tells Natalie what happened with her last living arrangement, just something about her roommate being a hormonal bitch.

"When I was pregnant I was a bitch, too," Suzi says.

"You were pregnant?"

"Yeah. I have a daughter."

"You do? Where is she?"

"She lives with her dad."

"Do you see her very often?"

"Sometimes."

"Do you have any pictures of her?"

"Somewhere," Suzi says, waving her hand in the direction of all her boxes and brimming black garbage bags.

"So you were married, then?" Natalie asks as they're driving to Lake Manawa.

"Yeah."

"Cooper's your married name?"

"Yeah."

"Do you guys get along?"

"Not really."

"So don't you miss your daughter?" Natalie asks on the way to work.

"I see her."

"What's her name?"

"Christine."

But in the month that Suzi has lived in Natalie's apartment there's been no daughter, no pictures of daughter, no phone calls to daughter, no visits.

The bachelor party is in a downtown penthouse apartment. From that height Natalie can look over the nothingness, the deserted nighttime streets of Omaha. She has a boom box and her special "Bachelor Party Mix" tape, an assortment of Public Enemy and Vanilla Ice and Salt-n-Pepa and Dee-Lite and 2 Live Crew.

The first bachelor party Natalie danced at she took her boyfriend du jour as bouncer. He took his video camera along with a duffle bag that she slowly filled with sweaty dollar bills. The party was pretty tame; she didn't even take off her top. Once the men realized she wasn't going to take off her top they just drank heavily and played pool. Although a bunch of them offered money to buy the video.

But Natalie isn't worried about a bouncer tonight, she knows these guys—she's worked at parties for them in the past. They're decent, for the most part. All firemen. They hoot and holler but always tip. And they keep their hands to themselves. She checks the address and rings the doorbell.

"You're here," the man who hired her says as Natalie waves. "Do you need a bathroom or someplace to change?"

"Yeah, thanks." She follows him through the house, past unfamiliar dancers walking around, sitting on men's laps, doing shots. "I didn't know there would be other dancers here."

"He wanted a big party. That's okay, right?"

"Oh yeah, no problem." The bathroom is already trashed with makeup bags and curling irons and Natalie changes into a pink g-string, fixes her face. She's never danced at a party with this many dancers. Usually it's just one or two. At least she won't have to work as hard. And she's being paid to be here regardless, $200 for two hours, plus tips.

The bachelor is sitting on the couch yelling at the television screen, one of those important fights, Mike Tyson or somebody. "Come sit down," someone calls. "What do you want to drink?"

Okay, Natalie thinks, so you're being paid to hang out and watch the match in a g-string. This might be the easiest party she's ever worked. Usually the men circle up and she's in the middle with her boom box. Usually the groom sits in the center for a few songs while she does her signature "rip the t-shirt off the groom's body and cover the shirt with lipstick kisses" routine. She always gives the ripped-up kiss-marked t-shirt to the best man to put on the wedding present table. Best men love that prank.

And usually she has to do a few lap dances. She might be able to get away with not doing them at the club, but at a bachelor party she can't avoid them. They vary from club to club and party to party, but usually they cost $20 and last the duration of one song. Sometimes they want her to back her ass up to their chests and wiggle it in their faces. Sometimes it's a face-to-face straddle that can go all the way to dry humping. Sometimes she can get away with just doing a little Egyptian dancy thing. The only thing she knows for sure is that she hates doing them, even if they're an industry standard, even if all the other girls do them, even if she ends up making less money at the end of the night because she doesn't do them. But at a party she can hardly avoid them. That's why she usually takes a bouncer.

The men watch the match while girls sit on their laps, fetch their drinks. Soon the doorbell rings and the cleaning lady enters the apartment: Mexican, mom-ish, short curly hair. *This late at night?* Natalie is embarrassed to be seen serving drinks in her pink g-string. But the woman doesn't seem shocked; she hardly looks Natalie's way.

Later, Natalie is on her way to the bathroom when she passes the open bedroom door and sees the woman still there. How weird. When she returns to her place on the couch, in front of the television, she asks, "What's that woman doing here? Did she not realize you were having a party?"

"She was hired."

"Hired?"

"Yeah, she's a sex addict and she'll have sex with everyone here and then she'll come out and masturbate herself to orgasm in front of everyone."

That woman? She looks like she should be making pot roasts in the kitchen. Even when Natalie starts noticing the men slip away one by one she doesn't want to believe it.

It isn't until she overhears one of the men whisper "...her sweet beaver..." to another guy that she realizes it's true. Natalie spots the bachelor coming from the bedroom, naked in the darkened hallway, his penis still semi-erect, talking to someone else. Negotiating.

Natalie leaves as soon as her two hours are over. She really doesn't want to see the woman masturbate herself to orgasm in front of them all. She now realizes why the men have been so tame all evening: they're getting off in the other room. Natalie and the others dancers are the eye candy foreplay, the beer-delivering afterglow. Natalie isn't sure how this makes her feel. She's the one getting the better deal, after all. Right? She's only being paid to watch television.

As Natalie comes out of the bathroom, dressed again, the woman is waiting in the hall, also fully dressed. Their eyes meet. Natalie is surprised to feel a slight twinge of disgust, the same disgust she will encounter later in congregations of women pontificating the evils of stripping.

But the Mexican woman with the short, curly hair looks at Natalie with a sort of sad camaraderie instead.

"I know what you've been doing. It makes me sick."

My father's words stick in my throat. "What are you talking about?

"I know about the *Sugar Lounge*."

"What do you mean?"

"I talked to a guy named Ralph. I told him you were only seventeen."

"My friend works there. I only went in to visit her."

"Sounds like you've picked really great friends."

I wish I had the courage to tell him to go to hell. I wish I had the nerve to call him a hypocrite.

After I hang up I start panicking. *What if he really did talk to Ralph? How will I show my face there again?* But it's Tuesday and there's an envelope of cash with my name on it in the boss's payroll drawer. I have to at least pick it up.

When I get to work I almost expect my father to be waiting outside, waiting to ground me like I was fourteen again. But no one says anything. Not the bouncer, the bartender, the owner—no one.

My father doesn't know my name is Natalie, I realize, as I go upstairs and undress for work. He doesn't know which one I am.

Stripper Tip #19: When a seventy-year-old customer asks if you want to go to Costa Rica, don't say yes just to get him off your back, because he's not going to forget and he's almost sure to show up at the club with a passport application, and then it's a real pain to avoid him.

Soon after Suzi moves in, Natalie comes home to find a blue pickup truck parked in front of her apartment building brimming with belongings. Bambi, another dancer and apparently Suzi's new best friend, is standing in the back of the truck. Natalie knows instinctually what's happening even before she sees Suzi carrying a cardboard box. Suzi and Bambi leave in a cloud of exhaust fumes. It isn't until she goes back into her apartment and takes inventory that she realizes Suzi has taken her Elsa Brown Modeling School tackle box.

Natalie takes the elevator to the 25th floor. This is the fanciest hotel in Omaha. She's never been in here before. She checks her reflection in the elevator walls: hair in place, makeup fresh, red lips, dangling hoop earrings, tight shirt.

Suite #243 has been turned into an office reception room. The official Playboy logo is everywhere: on banners, on pens, on the coffee cup in the receptionist's hand. Natalie is given an application with the official logo at the top.

Bust measurement?

Hip measurement?

Ethnicity? (Optional)

Do you want to pose: A: clothed, B: partially clothed, or C: nude?

Natalie checks all three. Thank god she's finally eighteen. What luck.

The other women waiting in line are nothing special. They look at Natalie like she's a shoe-in. Finally, for once in her life, she's a shoe-in. She'll sign photos at the magazine release party and meet Hugh Hefner. Maybe someday she'll be Miss December or Miss August.

The photographer comes out of the back room holding two Polaroid shots beginning to darken. He staples them to a piece of paper. Natalie is next. He looks at her and smiles. She can see the "yes" going through his mind. Her modeling background plus stripping background and even her pageant background—there will be no way they can refuse her.

The photographer sends her into the other room, a regular hotel room with a king-sized bed and a gaudy comforter and a few portable lights spotlighting the bed. "Should I get undressed?"

He holds up a finger as he looks over her application, leaves the room, and returns with another man who also looks her over. "You're eighteen?"

"Yes." She's actually legal now for things like R-rated movies and buying cigarettes and posing for Playboy.

"She's too young," one of them quietly says to the other. "When are you going to be nineteen?"

"I just turned eighteen. I thought Playboy's age was eighteen?"

"But this is the 'Girls of the Big 10,' so we have to follow state rules. In Nebraska the age is nineteen for nudity." He holds out his hand. "Maybe next year."

Natalie knocks on the door.

"I'm looking for Suzi."

"She's not here right now," Suzi's sister answers.

"Well, she just moved out of my apartment and took a bunch of my things. I need them back."

The sister doesn't seem terribly surprised by this. Natalie is escorted to the spare bedroom filled with all the boxes that just left her apartment. Natalie finds the Elsa Brown Modeling School tackle box right away. A quick glance over the piles yields Natalie's Lancome facial wash and lotion, her Fredrick's of Hollywood bustier. Her Rita Hayworth calendar. And she takes Suzi's goulash pot as payback.

Natalie puts all her stuff back in her car and waits in the living room. It is thrift store worn: frayed afghans on the corners of the couch, TV trays, a collection of ceramic dogs on the bookshelf. On the console television is a picture of Suzi holding a wrapped bundle. Natalie scoots closer. Suzi looks the same: wild brown curls though softer, face less tanned. The father is cut out of the picture. "That was the baby's christening," Suzi's sister says.

Natalie lifts the frame off the mantle. Suzi really does have a daughter. Natalie looks into the face of Suzi, scrubbed clean of makeup, smiling in that way a new mother smiles.

Stripper Tip #20: When you're dancing on stage and your high school principal, Father Frank Dimitri, comes into the club in street clothes and doesn't recognize you but you recognize him (you'd recognize that dyed hair and bushy monobrow anywhere) try not to look him in the eye when he tips you.

Natalie waits in the lobby of a Days Inn at two o'clock in the morning, flipping through a magazine. It's obvious what the hotel staff must think. How long should she wait before she leaves? *We're looking for a girl* they'd said in the darkened bar, just hours earlier.

They actually show up. The girl is smiling, even makes a comment about how they didn't think she would show. The three of them cluster around the reception desk like a big happy family, insisting on a room with a hot tub. It must be obvious. Into the elevator they go. Natalie doesn't pay much attention to the guy, a big silent hick with a big Nebraska gut. She's not thinking about him, she's thinking about the girl. She's thinking how nice it feels to be wanted.

In the suite they pull out a big bag of weed, start filling the hot tub. They seem pleasantly surprised by Natalie's eagerness. Natalie and the girl get in the tub, leaving him in the other room. They kiss, but as soon as Natalie reaches for her she suggests they invite the boy. He soon lowers his large body into the tub, making the water rise almost to the top.

They all go to bed, naked and warm from the hot tub. The girl disappears but the boy starts on her immediately, opens her legs and sticks his fingers in. His giant belly looms over her as his fingers dig there first. Then her ass. Natalie feels like a rag doll in his big arms. Soon he's on the bed and his warm, red dick is in her mouth and his red balls are hitting her chin and he's thrusting and cums in her mouth, hot and warm on the back of her throat.

And then she is finally there, spreading Natalie's legs, and he is gone, recovering, and Natalie feels the wash come over her, her first orgasm. She doesn't even know what happened.

And now he's back, looking eager, and Natalie suddenly excuses herself to the bathroom. I don't want to fuck that guy, she says to her stoned reflection in the bathroom mirror. I really don't want to be here anymore.

She quickly exits the bathroom and starts putting on her clothes. One glance into the darkened bedroom and she makes eye contact with the girl, who is sitting with her knees bent, legs open, while the boy thrusts into her like a big bear. Her eyes are half-closed, spacey as she watches Natalie leave.

XIV

You pass the XXX Adult Superstore. You park in the Love Shack's sprawling but mostly empty parking lot, next to a sedan with a baby seat in the back. Your hands are shaking. If Suzi is anywhere she'll be here, at the biggest, the best, the nudie-est. You approach the back of a gigantic peach building with a red stripe slicing its middle, solid and without windows, like the back of a supermarket. A tall antenna in the lot crackles with electricity. In all directions, empty fields and the buzz of cars on the interstate.

You open the black-painted glass door. You switchback through the metal lane dividers as if you're in line for a roller coaster. Through the turnstile. One barren ticket window. Everything feels efficient, bare, no frills, like they haven't been open long.

At the window you pay $20 to the middle-aged woman wearing a "Love Shack" polo shirt. She snaps a bracelet around your wrist. Further down a guy with long gray hair and apple cheeks shines a flashlight on your ID. "Here alone?" You give him the condensed version of your story. "Well then, do you remember me?" he asks. "I used to work the parking lot at the Sugar Lounge."

"I was there a *long* time ago, probably ninety-one, ninety-two."

"I was there." He gives his name but you don't remember him, though something in his goofy, maybe slimy, maybe sweet smile does look familiar.

You enter the vastness of the club like walking into a cathedral, the ceiling forever away. The stage begins in the distance, an alter that stretches into the darkness with a dozen golden poles. At the end of the stage is a girl, a tiny little dot on the horizon, wearing nothing but boots.

You continue to talk to the ex-parking lot attendant and buy a canned Heineken out of a cooler; other men are arriving with six-packs. As you crack your beer and head for one of the long foldout tables, the ex-parking lot attendant walks with you. "Who do you remember from those days?" he asks.

"Do you remember Suzi Cooper?"

He thinks while you take a sip of awful, canned beer. "Nope."

"How about Joe the bouncer?"

"Oh yeah, he's on kidney dialysis right now. Cecil died. You must have known Cecil then, too?" You nod. "Yeah, died in a car wreck."

"I heard Dick died, too."

"I went to his funeral. Lou Gehrig's disease."

"What about Alice?"

"Alice!" he chuckles. "I haven't thought about Alice in forever. I hear she still hangs out at the blah blah blah bar." He shakes his head. "I can't believe you remember Alice."

"Alice was great. She gave me my first shot of Goldschlager."

"Yeah." He's smiling and nodding. *Viva Alice, wherever you are.*

"You want me to show you around?" You nod, thankful to have a purpose in this cavernous place. "This is the shower. For twenty-five bucks you can watch 'em shower," he says as you pass a tiled stage and nozzle. Great idea, you think. You're seeing everything like a business person, now, thinking, Ol' Ralph's doing well for himself, good for him, as if you were being told about the tenure position of one of your college buddies.

"And these are the Champagne Rooms," he says, flipping on the light to a hallway with sixteen identical maroon curtains. In the office at the end of the hallway are sixteen identical screens showing sixteen empty rooms from different angles. You imagine all sixteen of those screens playing, each a little porn show while this guy watches for an illegal tip, a grope, a finger, a suck.

"On Saturday nights the whole place is packed. You

can hardly move." He switches off the light and returns you to the main room. "On Saturday nights we'll have all eighteen poles going," he says proudly.

"You look like Salma Hayek," he adds.

You end up at one of the picnic tables drinking your metallic beer. The girl onstage is naked and your eyes are drawn, like the eyes of everyone in here, to her tiny shaved beaver. The jewel in this cathedral. When she lays on the floor and opens her legs you see how her lips sparkle, like she swiped glitter gel on her crotch. You spend very little time looking at her face, her breasts, her extensive tattoos. You, like everyone else in here, are waiting for another flash of sparkle. You can't look away. Now two guys are at the lip of the stage. Her legs are open and she gyrates softly in front of them. Their eyes are glued to her sparkle.

You drink your beer quickly now, the third drink you've had in under two hours, when a man with white hair sits at your empty table.

"You're the one waiting for Ralph, right?"

"Uh, not really waiting, I'm just going to finish my beer."

"He won't be in until eleven, eleven-thirty. You probably don't want to wait that long."

"No, I'm not planning to wait that long."

"Yeah. I'm Ralph's brother." He holds out his hand and gives a firm handshake.

"Congratulations on the new club, I hear it's doing well."

"Oh yeah, it's doing well. I just came up from Florida to help open. I'm going back soon. I don't want to stick around here." He glances around.

You end up outside the building, smoking next to the garbage can ashtray in the fading light. Two men approach with six-packs, light their own cigarettes, make small talk about the smoking ban, you tell them you used to work for Ralph and one says, "Why even go in? I'll give you twenty bucks and you can dance for us right here." You laugh, sneer, funny, funny, and decide to leave. The car with the baby seat is still there as you go.

As I leave the Love Shack, the rain begins. I'm pretty drunk, driving very carefully in my little white minivan. I am the original wound. Biologically, I can only receive. I'm not built to intrude, only to be intruded upon. Women, we want to take. We want to take back. Biologically we can only receive. The original sparkly wound.

They don't understand the inherent vulnerability of a woman. They size me up, imagine how they would feel inside me, hope I'm tight enough, wet enough, hope I moan enough when they do me. But the pussy cannot *do*, no matter how encouraging the sex therapists and all the books might be. A woman on top is still a woman pierced, pinned and on display.

At least that's my experience of sex. I'm told there are others.

When I masturbate I dream of porn. It's the only way I know how to feel powerful. I picture straddling some faceless man in the dark corner of a nightclub. He slips his dick out through his zipper. I, nearly naked anyway, accept his $20 and pull aside the strip of fabric covering my crotch, sink over him and fuck him for the length of a song.

Or I'm on a bed, with cameras and lights all around. And the faceless dude with the movie-sized penis is flipping me over and fucking me. Maybe some of the cameramen get so hot that they put down the cameras and pretty soon I've got a dick in every opening and one in each hand.

Or it's some ugly, fat guy fucking me in some hotel room and I'm half disgusted but half turned on and his red balls are hitting my ass and there is a pile of money on the nightstand table and the fact that I know this makes me feel superior.

This is how I masturbate. Even to admit it makes me ill. I'm fucking the john or the cameramen or the guy in the suit with his cock poking through his pants, sucking on my nipple at no extra charge. Sex has always been my greatest commodity. I'll give you sex if you give me love. But eventually I stop wanting sex. My first orgasm was during a cheap threesome with two strangers, I spent my sexually formative years taking off my clothes for a living, I pimp myself for love the way my dad pimped my mom for self-esteem. This is how I was raised. This is all I know. No wonder I married a sex addict. He's more familiar to me than anyone else.

My hotel room has green carpet, dark wood furniture, a small refrigerator, microwave, one-cup coffee maker with filters. A spotless bathroom with towels that smell like hospitals. A television with too many channels, looping advertisements for porn. A very antique phone with red flashing light—message. Phone books, ads for the local pizza places, emergency numbers. It's been seventeen days since I saw my husband. I pick up the phone. Where are you? I tried your mom's house two days ago. I'm in Omaha. Why? It doesn't matter. How are the kids? Okay, confused. I talked with them when I called. Your mom sounded worried. Have you called her? Yeah. When are you going back? Tomorrow. What are you doing in Omaha? Visiting strip clubs. Why? I don't know. I wasn't telling you that I wanted you to leave. I couldn't stay. When are you coming back? I don't know. I'm not your father, you know. But you want me to be your fantasy woman. That's all I've ever been. No, I want you to enjoy it. But we're not friends. You're just not attracted to me. I've told you a hundred times that's not the issue. Then what? I'm just tired of taking care of other people's fantasies. I'm not *other people*. But it's always been about someone else. I need it to be about me, too. I love it when you're on top. But that's just an act. So you're just playing some kind of game with me? No. You're just keeping a tally. That doesn't help me, you know. So now you have to punish me? You don't get it. I've been punishing myself. I don't know who I am if I'm not someone's sex object. But it's been weeks since we had sex. It's like I'm looking at myself in a broken mirror and everything is skewed, all these pieces everywhere. You just don't like sex. Maybe you're a lesbian. Will you stop, please? We used to have a lot of sex at the beginning. Everyone does. Why should I have to pay for your sexual problems? Why should I have to pay for yours? I have needs, too. I need a *wife*.

And I need a friend.

You hang up slowly, soured with adrenaline. You've got to get out of this hotel room. Levon is just around the corner at an art showing for First Friday. You're grateful to have a destination that isn't a strip club and you rush around the block to find him in the back of a very crowded gallery. He hugs you so hard he cracks your back. You try to relax, admire his latest photos, guzzle wine. You buy a photo of a naked woman with angel wings standing in front of a large window. You've posed in front of that window.

After the art showing you both walk to the nearest restaurant. It's brick with exposed beams, Old Market style. "We have to get white pizza," you say. "You're the person who introduced me to it."

"Really?"

"Yep. It was white pizza with shrimp. You also introduced me to iced coffee and this honey lemon thing."

"The honey lemon thing. I must have been trying to seduce you," he says. "I forgot all about that."

Two tall beers arrive. You don't need to drink any more tonight but you click glasses with Levon.

"Thanks for coming out with me. You want to do a shot?"

"I'm too old for shots," he says, waving his hand. "It takes me three days to recover."

"Me, too." You order Patron.

"No leads on Suzi?"

You swallow the shot. Shudder. "Nope."

"She's toxic," Levon says. "Poisonous. Did I ever tell you what she did to me?"

"No."

"One time she had a shoot scheduled with me and she never showed up. A whole day wasted. So the next time she called me I said I wouldn't shoot her anymore. So she told everyone that I had tried to sleep with her."

"What?"

"Alice and all those girls shut her up immediately. They told her not to mess with me. She disappeared after that. Haven't seen her since."

"That sounds like Suzi. Toxic is the perfect word."

"I always knew you would turn out okay."

"I'm not sure if I did. I'm probably getting divorced when I go back home."

"That's not what I mean."

"I know."

"Hey," he says. "I know Suzi, remember? And if you really came all this way expecting something profound from that woman..."

"I know. I'm an idiot."

"When was the last time you saw her?"

"Years ago. At the club."

"And what happened?"

"As soon as I said 'you stole all my shit' we started yelling and then the bouncer made me leave."

"Joe?"

You pause. Where *did* that scene take place? It wasn't at the Sugar Lounge. Or Dick's. Or The Red Umbrella. "Levon," you say, "didn't there used to be another club right around the corner from here?"

"I can't keep track of them all anymore. Club 22?"

Club 22. How could you have forgotten Club 22? "*That's* the last place I saw her."

"Club 22" is spelled out in sparkly silver cursive along the side of the building. I skipped school again. If I skip too many times I won't graduate. I'll probably get called to the office tomorrow, but I don't care. Liberty told me to audition during the day. I hope she's here. The late spring day is cold, windy. I hope no one sees me. I open the door and go from the bright afternoon into a glittering den.

In the club it's always night. Natalie's heart pounds as Bambi holds open the door to Club 22. They enter the darkness, glitter and noise. Word on the street is that Suzi works here now. Natalie lets her eyes adjust to the darkness.

You're walking towards Club 22, stopping every half block so Levon can say hi to someone. The night is moist with a hint of cold coming. You leave the Old Market and walk east on 15th Street, remember how lonely downtown Omaha is. You see a few bums, a few tired-looking hookers. You recognize the Orpheum Theater and remember smoking in the alley, discovering the Club 22 billboard. Your very first audition was here, at Club 22, not at the Sugar Lounge like you've remembered it all these years. How could you have forgotten? You skipped school and everything.

I hide in the shadows. Maybe I should turn around and leave before anyone sees me? The place is completely empty, dead. How does Liberty make money here? I check my watch: 12:00 on the dot. No one has seen me—I should just turn around—oh no, that bartender just saw me. He's waving me over.

Natalie lets her eyes adjust to the darkness. Suzi is sitting at a table with a drink in her hand. She's wearing a long, sheer robe. "There she is."

"Where?" Bambi squints.

"There." Suzi's hair is still in that stupid banana clip. She's wearing a new costume under her coverlet, all red tassels. Who knows who she stole it from.

When Suzi sees Natalie she smiles, straight and white with the sliver of a gap between her two front teeth, a gesture so sweet and seemingly genuine that Natalie feels for a second like Suzi's really happy to see her. For a moment Natalie almost feels bad, wonders if she's doing the right thing.

"You stole a hundred and fifty bucks from me, out of my dresser drawer. And you stole a bunch of Natalie's shit." Bambi breaks the moment, purposefully loud, so all the customers can hear.

Suzi's look goes from adoring to icy. She glares at Bambi, then at Natalie, eye to eye now that she's wearing heels. "Fuck you," she says, coming at Natalie with a finger pointed. "You stole my mother's goulash pot."

"You stole a *bunch* of shit from me, Suzi. I had to go to your mom's house—"

"You're a liar —"

"Okay ladies, break it up," the bouncer says. He puts his hands on Natalie's shoulder and steers her out the door.

You cross the street and see the peeling silver letters: Club 22. No lights. The door doesn't budge. No hours are posted. Wow, it's closed down, you say to Levon. How could you have thought all these places still existed? After all, they're cleaning up downtown, moving all the smut out of the city. Your small life swept away with the rubble.

Liberty comes out of the dressing room. Thank god, I feel so out of place, here. Her blond hair is pinned softly away from her face and she's wearing a half-robe over her costume and super-high white heels. She looks perfect, just like Cheryl Ladd. Just like Miss America.

I wave and she meets me at the bar, towering in her heels. "You came," she says, surprised.

"Do you still think they're hiring?"

"Sure," she looks around for the owner. "Why don't I go tell him that you want to audition?"

"Great." My palms are totally sweaty. I can't believe I'm doing this. I hope they don't ask for my ID.

She returns with a slender, balding man. He holds out his hand. "She wants to audition," Liberty says by way of introducing us.

"Did you bring a costume?"

"No, uh..."

"I have something she can wear." Liberty grabs my arm. "Follow me."

The dressing room is tiny, a hovel with an old mirror and an overflowing counter. She holds up the skimpiest bikini I've ever seen, "You'll look great in this." My god, I didn't shave enough to be able to wear that. I have no choice but to dry shave with her disposable razor. "Did you bring shoes?"

"No."

"I have some."

I step into her crazy black contraption with only enough fabric to cover my nipples and crotch. As she ties the strings behind my back I spot her Elsa Brown Modeling School tackle box on the counter. It's the only familiar thing in the room.

She leads me out to the stage. I climb the stairs and Liberty asks me, "What kind of music do you like?" and all I can do is dry swallow and tell her to pick anything and she's yelling out band names and I tell her to just pick something, anything to fill the awful silence. My hands are clammy when I grip the brass pole, trying not to look in the multiple mirrors, including the one over my head. I'm walking on a mirror, too. I can't look anywhere. I don't feel sexy. I feel like a fat, white, pasty cow wearing a slingshot.

Approximately thirty seconds later I give back the costume and shoes and I can't leave fast enough, even as the owner is trying to figure out if I can work on Wednesdays or Saturdays, and I say anything, anything at all just to get out the front door, knowing I will never come back.

XV

The dumpster groans as it slams shut, Natalie's red-spiked heels and rhinestone bustier silenced forever. She imagines the bum who will discover the duffel bag full of worn costumes and four years of her life, salvaging the bag from among the piles of garbage. When he opens it the smell of the bar will engulf him: perfume mixed with hairspray, stale smoke, shoes worn without socks. Maybe he'll lift out a costume, sniff at the crotch. Maybe he'll find a forgotten dollar bill tied around one of the straps like a stiff green corsage. Maybe he'll think about a stripper he hasn't thought about in years, a woman who used to make him feel less lonely, a woman who used to greet him with a smile like she was happy to see him. He remembers this woman more fondly than he does his ex-wife. In some strange way he even loved her.

XVI

As I'm driving away from Omaha I see it: Suzi's Showgirls.

It's a stretch, I know, but I'll probably never be back.

I sit at the bar and order a Pepsi. I'm the only customer. It's a strange sanctuary in the middle of the afternoon. The place is empty. A dancer comes out of the dressing room for her set. There's an easy banter between her, the owner, and the bartender. I forgot how it is during lunch, so laid back.

She has long blond hair and fake, grapefruit boobs. Seventeen years ago fake boobs were rare. She's bored; there's no one in here. She kneels on the stage, gives me ten or fifteen seconds worth of jiggly cleavage shots, then wanders to the rear of the stage where she can lean against the mirror. She spins around the pole out of routine, like a little kid swinging around monkey bars, her eyes glazed, mind elsewhere. She even gets down off the stage at one point, walks over to a cup of coffee sitting at the bar, takes a big swig, and brings it with her and leaves it within reach of the stage.

The cocktail waitress refills my barely touched Pepsi. "Are you meeting someone?" she asks.

"Sort of. I'm looking for a dancer named Suzi Cooper."

"You mean the owner's girlfriend?"

My heart almost stops. "Really?"

"She's bartending later tonight."

I can hardly keep from throwing up from the sudden anxiety of it all. "Does she have dark curly hair?"

"Yeah."

"She's short, smiley..."

"Yeah, yeah."

"What time does she come in?"

"She'll get here around five or so."
I check my watch. It's 12:20.

It's 1:00 when I skitter across the cobblestones of Old
Market, buzzed on caffeine. In four hours I'm going to see
Suzi. My stomach hurts. What will I say to her?

Since it's lunchtime I head to the Spaghetti Factory, for
old time's sake. The exposed beams are painted burgundy
and forest green, the smell of garlic in the air. I already
know what I'm going to order. I always get the same thing
at Spaghetti Factory.

At the salad bar I praise the Midwest, where you can
still get ham cubes with peas and black olives and mashed
up hard boiled eggs. Other Omahans are dousing their
salads with ranch dressing, then thousand island on top
of that.

When my plate is brimming with Nebraska fixins and
two kinds of dressing I return to the table. My booth looks
over the cobblestone intersection, Nebraskans shuffling by
in red football t-shirts and baseball hats. I once read that
on game days the Cornhusker stadium becomes the third
largest city in Nebraska.

The waitress arrives with my order: thick noodles
swimming in garlic and olive oil. My father and I ate this
every time we came to the Old Market. Once you finish your
plate, you send it back and order a second. You can even
switch up the sauces: white clam, red clam, meat marinara,
vegetarian. No matter how full we were my father and I
always ordered a second plate just on principle. One of the
last times I saw him was here.

I drink another iced tea, pay my tab. Head down a
lesser-traveled Old Market street. Around every corner I
anticipate the ghost of Suzi, tossing her hair and checking
her reflections in all the windows. And me, searching for
the right words: You told me you had a daughter but I didn't
believe you, never saw any proof, I knew nothing about you

except you were female and willing, before that you were just another trashy girl in a banana clip. Maybe I wanted to eat a pussy so I could say that I had. Maybe you chose me for the same reason, shiny parts on display. We were men's girls, not lesbians, our place was dolled up and on stage. Maybe I wanted to see myself the way they saw me. Maybe you didn't have a penis but we were still operating under the same fucked up rules, like fish immersed in polluted water.

And yet the one time we had sex, real sex, when we were alone and not in a threesome or an orgy or a sex club, it was nice. You seemed to tolerate me at best and it wasn't until all the dildos had been put away and you curled against me like a tiny baby that I felt something like love, though not love, but something.

But you fucked it all up because you were fucked up too, and so all I got was another version of my father, this one with a vagina. Having sex with you couldn't set me free. I hated women so I hated you, but you surprised me, you hated me back, and so there we were, two glamour girls vying for who gets to be on top. Two glamour girls trying to possess in each other what we had already forfeited in ourselves.

"Are you here for the amateur contest?" the doorman at Suzi's Showgirls says as he stamps my hand. I blush and shake my head.

Christina Aguilera is singing "makes me just a little bit stronger, makes my skin a little bit thicker," when I walk in the door. Beefy bouncer types with earpieces stand at the end of the hallway to double-check IDs. They're young, probably in college. Everyone looks so young.

She's wiping down the bar. All her long curly hair is swept up into a poofy ball at the crown of her head. She's wearing a long-sleeved black button-down shirt, several buttons unbuttoned, and a gold pendant that hangs between her new cleavage. Gold hoops and frosted lipstick. She's still looks good, trashy but beautiful the way she always has.

The bar is mostly empty. I watch my reflection in the mirror behind the bottles. When she greets me I see the sparkle of a diamond nose piercing.

"What can I get for you?" she shouts, leaning over the bar close to my face to hear me over the music, giving me a full tanned silicon cleavage shot.

"Crown and ginger ale." My stomach is flipping.

She nods and packs a glass full of ice. She holds the bottle of Crown high in the air, a perfect stream of gold splashing over ice, then sprays it with soda and sets it in front of me. "Twelve dollars."

I give her my credit card. Tone Lōc is saying "she loves to do the wild thing."

Should I tell her? She takes my card to the cash register. I do the math. If she was twenty-three when I was seventeen that would make her forty now. She looks good for forty. Her black polyester pants are tight, shirt tucked in so I can see the familiar shape of her ass. Lest I get too nostalgic, I remind myself the only reason I'm so familiar with the shape of her body is because I watched her dance on stage every night for years. Well, maybe one year. Shit, maybe it was even less than a year. I'm running through my timeline when she's back, wiping the still-clean bar in front of me with a wet rag. She lifts my drink and the napkin and wipes, then sets them back down. The dry paper napkin sticks to the now moist countertop. I reach for my latest pack of cigarettes and slam them against my palm with far more emphasis than needed, unravel the gold string and the plastic and yank out the aluminum inside. Lift a cigarette to my mouth and she's right there with a perfect teardrop of flame.

There are other people at the bar, but it's not busy. Suzi paces, smiles, wipes other patches in front of other customers. She moves as if she's used to being watched.

I know that role. It's as familiar to me as the shape of her muscular ass behind those polyester pants.

She starts chatting with someone at the other end of the bar. If I left Omaha when I turned eighteen, then the last time I saw her I was less than eighteen. So we must have met the year I was seventeen. Could our whole relationship have taken as little as six months? Four months? I can only recall a few scenes:

1. Going to Lake Manawa and her being asked to leave because she was wearing a thong.

2. Going to Popeye's Fried Chicken after I had become addicted to red beans and rice.

3. Going to the Fredrick's of Hollywood store at the mall.

4. Going to Joe's Fish Shack, her favorite place to eat popcorn shrimp.

5. Doing that one bachelor party together.

6. When she took me to her mother's house to pick up some clothes.

Can I have based an entire relationship on these things?

Suzi's back. "You want another one?" she asks, taking my empty glass.

She's right, I just chugged that. Nerves. I nod.

"Are you doing the amateur contest?"

"Oh, no." I wave the suggestion away, laughing.

She looks me over. "Are you from Omaha?"

I shake my head, suck down my drink, order another. The bar is empty, so she wipes the bar in front of me again. She replaces my barely wet cocktail napkin with a dry one. "Let's do a shot while you think about it."

"Think about what?"

"The amateur contest."

"Hell no." I look away and exhale. "You've got to be crazy."

"Winner gets a free trip to Puerto Rico. It's not like you're going to see any of these people again."

It must be the alcohol talking because I say, "I'll think about it."

She pulls out a metal mixer and strains a concoction into two rocks glasses. We clink. She still gets her nails done, I notice while she throws back her drink and I gulp, gulp, gulp, trying to keep up.

"Thanks," I say. "What was that?"

"I call it Sex on the Beach and a Fuck in the Ass." She smiles. I'm glad she never fixed that gap between her two front teeth. "So what are you doing in Omaha?"

"Looking for someone."

"Who?"

"A dancer."

"She works here?"

"I don't know. She used to work in Omaha but I guess it's been too long."

"How long?"

"Nineteen ninety-two."

Suzi chuckles. "Yeah, good luck." She empties the ashtray. "You were a dancer?"

"Yeah."

"You must have been young. Does she owe you money?"

"No."

"Steal your man?"

"No."

One of the dancers comes up to the bar with a wad of ones. "Forty," she says, handing the bills to Suzi in a carefully folded pile like a drug deal. Suzi counts them into the drawer and I check out her high-heeled boots. I forgot how short she is.

She hands the dancer two $20 bills and closes the drawer. Now she's back in front of me, just in time to dump my still-clean ashtray.

"That girl's turning tricks. As soon as I catch her I'm firing her skanky ass."

"I guess some things never change."

Suzi reaches for her own pack of...yes, Marlboro 100s. We share an ashtray. "Now they're proud of it. When I was a dancer it still happened, but you weren't proud of it."

I flick the end of my cigarette so hard the cherry falls in the ashtray. I try to pick it back up with the end of my cigarette, coax it back on. She helps another customer and I suck down half my drink. My legs are wobbly.

She must know.

I don't think she knows.

She has to know.

She doesn't seem to know. It *has* been seventeen years. I look through the club, trying to find a dancer that looks like I did. The one on stage, maybe? Or that girl over there— big boobs like I would have had before breastfeeding. Or her? Thigh-high stockings. Tasseled costume. I could have been any of them.

A new dancer is climbing the stairs to the stage. The old guy sitting next to me is watching her too. She raises her leg to the side like a dog peeing and shows her crotch, then she rubs her breasts together and touches the erect nipple with her tongue.

He turns to me, "I don't like that one." He has a French accent. His hair is white.

"I don't think she's been dancing very long," I say. "See how stiff she is?"

He guffaws into his drink. "She would make love with no heart."

I look at her again and chuckle. He's right.

"Do you want another one?" Suzi interrupts.

I'd stopped paying attention to Suzi. My cigarette has a long, delicate ash. "I'm fine, thanks."

"You let me know when you're ready." She wipes the counter again. "You never told me why you were looking for your friend."

She always knew how to engage me. I turn away from the stage. "Maybe I just wanted to see how everything turned out."

She shakes her head. "Let me tell you something," she crushes her cigarette, leans in closer to me, gestures with her long red fingernail, "I see women come in here all the time with their boyfriends or husbands, all shy at first. By the time they leave you always know they're going to go home and fuck the shit out of their men."

"Yeah."

"Did you like being a dancer?"

"I told myself I liked it."

She rolls her eyes. "What's that supposed to mean? You either liked it or you didn't."

"I liked it."

"Well," she says, "you want to see how everything turned out? Get up there."

I don't say anything.

"I'll give you fifty bucks to enter that contest."

She squints, stares at me.

"What, I suppose you have a husband now. Kids too, right?"

I feel the blood rush to my face.

"You too good for us now, *Natalie?*"

She lays a $50 bill on the counter and pushes it towards me. I look at it. I picture the entire scene: the dressing room, the counter covered with abandoned curling irons crusted with brown hairspray, eyeshadow and blush ground into the formica. Stretch marks lacing my butt and upper thighs like delicate vines, breasts a little softer. Random gray hairs shining silver among the dark.

I can feel the cool air on my skin as I climb the steps to the stage in my Joe Boxer panties and lacy bra. My history is written on my body. But under the red lights, history is washed away. My face is softened, teeth whitened, hair dark and shadowy. This is the Natalie she would remember, this fuzzy, angelic ghostlike version of myself.

I'm warming up, feel the drug of attention begin to pulse through my body. Lean against the mirror, rock my hips from side to side, slide all the way down to eye level.

Muscle memory comes back instinctively as I undulate shoulders-chest-pelvis-thighs in a slow body ripple all the way down to the floor, then all the way back up to standing. My thighs shake, reminding me that I'm out of practice, but my body remembers.

Two men ante up bills on the stage. I bend down and hear my knees crack. And laugh. Fuck it.

I imagine the French guy coming up to me, looping a bill through my panties saying, "There is no contest, you are the best one here." I imagine the applause-o-meter finale, each girl stepping forward to receive her score, and when I step forward a deep ocean wave of applause builds, then comes rushing towards the stage like everyone has been waiting to cast their vote until now.

I'm imagining it all as Suzi whips up two tequila shots, salt, lime. This is probably all novelty to her. She probably hasn't thought about me in years. I bet her version of the story is totally different. Maybe she doesn't even remember the last time we saw each other, when I had to be escorted out by a bouncer. Or maybe she remembers but doesn't care.

"Do you ever miss being on stage?" I finally ask.

She shrugs. "I make more money behind the bar. Less hassle."

"But do you think it affected you?"

"In what way?"

"I don't know, like sex is always a performance or something?"

She thinks about that for a minute. "Sex is always a performance. I don't believe in romance, if that's what you mean. You're the hearts and flowers type. You wanted to believe that everyone who ever fucked you was in love with you."

"I was only sixteen."

Now she's surprised. "You were?"

"Yeah, maybe seventeen by the time we met." I dig for my driver's license and offer it for inspection.

She's scrutinizing it and shaking her head and smiling at me in a way that almost feels like respect. "Wow."

Now she grabs the $50 bill, holds it out to me. "Here, this is yours. Unless you're planning to chicken out."

I reach for it. Pause. Withdraw.

"You know what? Buy a new goulash pot. We'll call it even."

You enter the warmth of Levon's building, round the familiar crumbly hallway and through the green door into his studio.

Do you want anything? he yells from the kitchen.

I need some water.

He comes out of the kitchen with two waters. Here, sit your butt down and I'll show you some of my new stuff.

You're thankful for the distraction. You don't really feel like talking. Levon takes you through his new pictures: gorgeous woman on four-poster bed; tattooed woman on hardwood floor; laughing woman in handcuffs with wild, beautiful hair. No sparkling vaginas, no pink patina of airbrushing like in the girlie mags.

This woman here, she's fifty-four years old. She's absolutely breathtaking, just breathtaking. Look at the light coming through the window in this one. Isn't it just stunning?

Oh, this is Elf. Elf is so gorgeous and she doesn't even know it. Look at those eyes. He flips to a picture of blue eyes heavily lined in kohl. Those eyes just make you want to die. I love her dimples. She's so delightful, so fun to shoot, too. This is Sandy, he says with reverence. She's stunning. Look at that. He flips to a photo of a gorgeous woman in an antique chair next to a corner window. That was such a fun day. It was raining and I was trying to shoot her and then, at the perfect moment, the sun came through just a touch and look, he holds his breath as he flips to a perfect sunbeam. Isn't it gorgeous?

You nod. It is gorgeous.

Do you still like your body? he asks.

You look at the computer screen, trying to seem nonchalant.

He stops and stares at you. It's so good to see you again. Let me look at you. He takes your face in both of his hands. You're all grown up, now, he says.

Your eyes fill with water. It's the alcohol, *for god's sake don't start crying now*. But it's too late, the water is filling and spilling over and all you can do is hug him and hope he doesn't see, but right away he's saying, "I'm sorry, I didn't mean to make you cry," and you're laughing and sniffling and saying "It's okay, it's good. Happy crying," and you hug and he rocks you and when you go to the bathroom he laughs and you yell "What's so funny?" while blowing your nose and he says, "Oh, nothing, just us," and when you return you realize he's been crying too. You wonder if either of you will ever know the reason behind the other's tears.

XVI

Early next morning the sun fills the room, softened by gauzy curtains. I stretch into the cool areas of the bed, revel in my aloneness. Something has lifted, though I can't put my finger on it. It doesn't have a name but I know it existed because I feel its absence.

Omaha glistens. People are wearing red Nebraska sweatshirts; it must be game day. It's chilly but fresh after all the rain. I walk along a canal and remember a photo shoot next to it, something for Elsa Brown, I think. I try to remember where that picture might be buried now, in some trunk at home.

I wander happily through the tents of the farmer's market like a little girl. On the corner a woman plays a harp. While the Old Market hasn't escaped the plague of lofts, the corner of 14th and Jackson looks the same, the freshly painted trolley just as I remember. Other restaurants have changed hands, the used record store is gone, the European Bakery has expanded into one of the old bookstores. But the shoe-buffed cobblestones are the same; my ten-story apartment building still has the faded words "O'Keefe's Meat Packing" on the red brick.

I pass the fruit and flower vendor, the cigar cart, the horse and carriage a la Dickens, the man with a handlebar moustache, the French Café with its never-ending tiki flame thrashing under a corrugated tin awning.

Then I'm driving away, past the Bohemian Café, Howards Mexican restaurant, the Henry Doorly Zoo and Rosenblatt Stadium. Past John Cougar Mellencamp A-frames, little pink houses for you and me. Between the trees are glimpses of the Missouri River, the old make-out spot. Past the dilapidated American Family Inn, the abandoned Southroads Shopping Mall, eclipsed by the bigger, newer malls in the suburbs. The Skateland where

I used to go on Saturdays and had my first sexual urges, always for the older ones, the ones who looked like they could take my hand and lead me through life like a couple-skate, backwards. Skateland is now a warehouse of granite tabletops and kitchen tiling. The Ben Franklin craft store is a now a Dollar Tree. That quirky Italian restaurant where my family used to get pizza is now a Grease Monkey.

I drove by my childhood house last, almost didn't go at all. I drove slowly, stalking the streets of the leafy, overgrown neighborhood and inched around the old cul-de-sac, remembering children I babysat and boys I loved. The tree in front of our old house was gone. Among all those trees my house was exposed, naked in the bright sunshine.

Acknowledgments

I wouldn't be the writer I am without E.B. Giles, Bryan Jansing, Benjamin Dancer, Kona Morris, Leah Rogin-Roper, Katharyn Grant, and Ronica Roth, my dearest colleagues and friends, who not only encouraged me but helped me refine, rework, and polish this story to a shine.

My sincere gratitude to Remy, who took this journey with me. Also to Beth Strong for midwiving me through the birth of this story. To Nate Jordon and Monkey Puzzle Press, who saw the sparkle in these pages. Thanks to Selah Saterstrom, Danielle Dutton, Adam Seth, Drew Hetzel, Patrick Robel, Justin Kulyk, Andrew Wille and everyone at the Jack Kerouac School of Disembodied Poetics who worked on this manuscript in its various incarnations. Thanks to: Andrew, Dan, Jill, Erich, Erik, Toby, Daphne, Andrea, Michael, Liv, Aerial, Sally, Chris, Fattie B, Belizbeha, Alicia and Doug, The Rennies, Scott, Rick, Niki, Laurieann, Brett, The Huerfano Community, Fast Forward Press and everyone who inspired, supported and listened to me endlessly. Special thanks to Johanna Gallers, who is still challenging me.

Thanks to my parents, who gave me both the love and the obstacles I needed to become the woman I am today. Thanks to my children, Van and Felix, who continue to teach me. And my deepest thanks to Nick, for everything...